MW01136676

ISBN: 978-1796472929

COMPLEX

Rose Fresquez

To Elizabeth Proske. Thanks for everything!

To my Lord Jesus Christ, who makes everything possible.

CHAPTER 1

Detective Trevor Freeman sat in the interview room and wiped the perspiration that threatened to flood his dark skin. He wiggled in his seat to take off his olive green jacket and observed the victim who'd been robbed while working at his uncle's store.

"Aidan, do you have any questions before we proceed?"

"Uh ... I'm good, I guess." Aidan rubbed the back of his neck with his hand.

Trevor rose from his seat and gave the seventeen-year-old a friendly pat on the shoulder. Being only nine years older, Trevor hoped his youthful appearance would put the guy at ease.

"Are you ready to view the lineup of the suspects?"

Aidan nodded his response and followed Trevor to another room.

"Do you see the men who robbed the store?" Trevor asked, while his partner Enrique observed.

Aidan's gaze narrowed as he studied the row of men behind the glass, his fingers tapping on his cheek. He turned to Trevor. "Number two for sure," he said. "He was holding the door with a baseball bat in his hand."

Trevor took a step closer, thankful that this case was coming to an end. "Anyone else?"

Aidan gazed through the glass. "Hmm ... I want to say it's number four," he said, pointing to the guy with long hair dyed in neon colors. "He looks like the dude who jammed the gun in my ribs while I was hanging screwdrivers on the display rods. But he didn't have piercings, or dyed hair."

Trevor and Enrique exchanged looks.

"Let's go with the one with piercings and dyed hair," Trevor spoke, confident that was the guy he needed. He had a gut feeling.

"What if ... he's not the one?" Aidan asked.

"That's not for you to stress about," Trevor said. "We'll bring him in for questioning, and if he's not the one, we'll let him go."

Trevor was ninety-eight percent certain the suspect with dyed hair was one of the robbers. For one thing, he could have just dyed his hair as a disguise. Two, from the way the piercings on his nose were swollen and bleeding it looked as if he'd just gotten that done a few days ago.

Two hours later, after questioning, it turned out that the two suspects knew each other and had robbed the hardware store. It had been easy to get the guy with dyed hair to confess since he panicked when Trevor told him he was going to stay in jail for two years. Trevor had told him if he made it easier by admitting his guilt, his sentence would be shortened.

This had been the second case Trevor had solved this week. He was in a good mood for the rest of the afternoon at work and as he drove home at the end of the day. Since his colleague Enrique had the night shift, Trevor hoped to at least get home in time to get a few things done.

As he drove towards home, Trevor's good mood was interrupted when a red mustang crept over the center-line. Trevor cursed under his breath as he swerved and skidded to a stop.

He pulled his speedometer and clocked the car at fifteen miles over the speed limit. Unfortunately, he knew that car and the driver, since he'd given him a speeding ticket two days ago. Brent Wise. Just thinking of the name stirred some memories of his mom that he'd tried to set aside and move on.

Since Trevor's duties as a small-town detective included more than solving mysteries, he sighed and raked a hand through his black, tight curly hair before turning on his red and blue lights to chase after the car.

"Do you know how fast you were going?" Trevor asked when Brent rolled down the window.

"Just give me the darn ticket," Brent snapped. "You think giving me tickets will rectify your mom's disappearance?"

Trevor wouldn't say they'd ever been friends, due to more reasons than just the fact that his mom used to be their housekeeper before she went missing.

"I'm going to give you a warning, this time."

Brent's contemptuous gaze lingered on Trevor's feet. "Just give me the ticket. Looks like you could use a new pair of shoes anyway."

Even if Trevor could use a new pair of shoes, that was the least of his concerns at the moment. "You can only get so many tickets before your license is suspended."

"Are we done here?" Brent asked. "Unlike you, I have other important things to do."

Trevor's jaw tightened, and he bit his lip, holding back the words that he wanted to say. He forced himself to wave at Brent and moved back to his SUV, the one the town's people had bought for the police. He had no doubt that the Wise family had contributed some funds as well.

Brent's words bothered him all the way home, stirring up a longing for his mom. Who did the Wises think they were? He pulled into the driveway of his childhood home, the one he'd always known, and which he now shared with his dad Rex and sister Keisha.

As Trevor settled back on his pillow that night, he tossed and turned several times before he pulled himself out of bed. He powered his laptop and went to the kitchen to make himself a coffee. He returned to the living room shortly with a steaming mug and went back to the email his friend Dan, had sent him two weeks ago, with a picture of his mom.

He sat on the couch shuffling through the files on his computer as he nursed a cup of coffee in the dimly lit living room of the three-bedroom house.

By studying at night, he didn't inconvenience his dad, Rex and his sister, Keisha, plus the darkness helped him concentrate. He glanced at the lit clock on the wall. A little after midnight, and if his father knew he was going through these records, he would blow a lid.

His gaze narrowed on the picture in his file of a woman who looked like his mother, studying it with interest. With each click of the mouse and turn of the pages in the case file, he was trying to be as quiet as possible. The last thing he wanted was to wake up his family and face their scrutiny. They didn't exactly approve of the sleepless nights he spent investigating their mother's disappearance.

His dad, Rex, did better when it came to the whole 'let bygones be' and leaving vengeance to the Lord. But Trevor did not let things go without putting up a fight. As a new believer, Trevor was starting to let

God fight his battles, but that was easier to accept when he didn't think so much of his mom. Besides, he often wondered, wasn't there also a saying that God helped those who helped themselves? Perhaps this was his way of helping himself—seeking justice for his mother.

Dad had told him to lay off the case for a while. He insisted it was consuming Trevor, and that he was becoming obsessed with the case.

His family made it clear that they thought he couldn't do anything with his life because of it, but Trevor had found that idea ridiculous. After all, he was the town's detective. If Trevor helped investigate other cases, why not use the skills for his family's benefit? He could admit that he was obsessed, but who wouldn't be obsessed with finding their mother if she went to work one day and never came back?

He let out a long sigh. Nothing seemed to make sense, and the case had only gotten more complicated. Convinced that his mother, Jayla's employers had something to do with her disappearance, Trevor had filed a lawsuit against them, five years ago. If he could only find enough evidence to make this more of a case than just a made up story he would ....

The Wises thought they were above anyone else who wasn't in their wealthy circle. And that was one thing Trevor couldn't stand.

The arrogance of that family was beyond what he could handle. He couldn't fathom how people could be so careless. They didn't even seem fazed by his mother's disappearance. It was too bad they messed with the wrong person—they would not get away with this. If his suspicions proved correct, he would make sure they paid for their crimes.

After all his mom had done for them, working hard as their housekeeper, for them to not even bat an eye at her disappearance was unsettling. Trevor knew the family was self-centered, but he'd never imagined anyone could be so cold.

Although Trevor may have found himself consumed with the task of solving his mother's case, it was only because he wouldn't be able to live with himself if Jayla became one of those news stories of a woman who went missing without a trace. Whether she was alive or—as much as it pained him to think about it—dead, he needed closure. He was going to get to the bottom of it, regardless of how many toes were stepped on in the process.

"You still looking at mama's case?" a soft female voice asked from somewhere in the darkness.

Trevor raised his head up from the files he had been mulling over. He could just make out the form of his little sister. Her petite figure was leaning against the wall that separated the kitchen from the living room, observing him. Her jet-black hair was knotted into a loose ponytail.

Keisha had been about thirteen years old, and Trevor twenty-one when their mother had disappeared. While Keisha remembered the woman, she probably didn't have as strong of a bond with her as Trevor had. Though she had cried and mourned the absence of their mother, Keisha had long ago come to the conclusion that their mother was dead and was never coming back.

A conclusion Trevor refused to subscribe to about the mother he remembered so well.

The detective side of him knew that something had likely gone wrong with his mom, but this wasn't just a case of a stranger gone missing. This was his mom! There had been many cases over the years of people being held hostage for years. She could still be alive.

His gaze briefly returned to the picture in his hand, and he considered putting it back in the file so he could look it up another day. "Yes, Ki," he finally responded. "What's up?"

"Felt thirsty, came to get some water, and almost thought I wouldn't find you still awake, but you're always up late, doing the same thing." She offered a weak smile. "Disappoint me for once, Trev."

Keisha might have rolled her eyes at the end of her sentence but the light was too dim for Trevor to see her eyes. He shook his head, letting her words slide off.

She was starting to sound too much like their father these days.

"You had your water?" he asked, effectively dismissing anything else she had said. He wasn't going to engage her in this argument at such a late hour. Besides, whenever he did have this argument, it never led to a resolution. Only frustration for both parties.

Keisha was silent for a while, but Trevor waited for her response.

"Yes," she responded reluctantly. However, he didn't miss the slight defiance in her voice. Trevor could read his sister better than he could read anyone else. He'd taken care of Keisha since she was a baby, from helping his mom change her diapers to entertaining her. He'd watched her grow from infancy to the full teenager she was, and when their mother went missing, he had more or less taken over part of the parenting role alongside his dad.

Trevor was a lot like a second parent, and his knowledge of Keisha was just as apt as any parent would have of their child. He knew she wanted to help him. She meant well. They all did.

"Goodnight Ki, you better get to bed." he said gently, dismissing her.

Once again, she stood silent for a minute longer before making any action, and then turned. "You might want to consider your own advice and catch some sleep," she spoke over her shoulder. "Your endless worrying is catching up on you." Keisha offered those last parting words before disappearing into the shadows from where she'd emerged.

Trevor looked at the file in his hands, only this time, he wasn't really seeing the pictures, just staring at them as he thought of Keisha's words. He wiped his hands across his heavy eyes, closed up the file, and tossed it onto the coffee table with a grunt. He gulped the rest of the coffee in his cup. It was a hopeless effort, as the coffee had been ineffective in blocking his exhaustion, but drinking the bitter liquid had become part of his ritual.

Turning off the lights, Trevor made his way to his bedroom. Keisha was right—he barely got any sleep these days, and his exhaustion was catching up to him. Sleepless nights poring over his mother's case and preparing for the trial left him tired at work in the mornings. He just needed this case solved. Six years was too long to be put through this level of emotional torture and pain. He needed his mother back, and a specific member of the Wise family in jail for abducting her.

CHAPTER 2

Sofia Wise finger-combed her blonde hair just as the landing strip came into view and the plane descended to land. It had been a long time since she'd been in Colorado— a little over ten years.

Homecoming left her with a nostalgic feeling that she was sure would only get worse the closer she got home. She grew uncomfortable as memories flooded her mind because there were pieces of her past she wasn't yet ready to face. Everything was different now, and if it weren't for a terrible turn of events, she wouldn't be returning home just yet.

The reason for her sudden return was her grandmother Eunice's death. Eunice had been the glue that bonded the family together, and she'd been more of a mother to Sofia than her own parents had been. The ache of her loss was too much to bear. Sofia felt saddened for having missed the funeral, since Eunice had died while Sofia was on a trip to Burundi, Africa. She'd gone with a couple of friends, teaching English to students for three months, and they'd been in a primitive village with no electricity or phone service. Not that she would have contacted home if she'd had the service, but it would have been beneficial to get first-hand news of her grandmother's passing.

Now that Eunice was dead, Sofia wondered what everyone at home would be like. Would they be grieving her death? Would this death bring some humanity back to her family? She'd spoken to her mom three weeks ago, and they'd agreed to do a post-funeral service and visit the gravesite whenever Sofia got home. She'd been a bit relieved that her mom had seemed excited at the prospect of seeing her. Not knowing what her dad thought about her visit was another issue altogether—one she was hesitant to face.

The plane finally came to a stop, and most of the passengers started the hustle and bustle of making their exit, while others trudged through for their carry on pieces of luggage from the overhead bin. Sofia took her time and let the rush pass by before she reached for her own carry-on luggage.

Her eyes scanned the crowd as she made her way through the terminal, where she immediately spotted her brother leaning against the wall, his eyes glued to a cell phone. Still lean and handsome with his trimmed, sandy blonde hair slicked to the side. She didn't have to look at his eyes to remember they were green like hers.

If she remembered anything about Brent Wise, it was his punctuality; and perhaps that came with the nature of his profession as the next CEO of Wise Enterprise.

She snuck up to Brent, stood on her tiptoes and whispered close to his ear, "Hey, stranger!"

Brent jumped and spun around. "Sofie!" he greeted her with a smile. Brent put his phone in his pocket before he embraced her in a hug. "Welcome home."

Sofia hadn't kept in touch with her brother as much as she would have liked, except for once a year when she'd call him for his birthday. Brent was older by four years, and with their clashing personalities, they'd spent more time fighting than bonding. She'd missed her brother though, and she hoped they'd connect during her visit.

"It's good to be home," she said.

Brent turned away. "Let's get your luggage."

The Colorado sun hit Sofia's skin as soon as they stepped outside, but it was nothing compared to the heat of the remote village she had been staying in. Sofia smiled to herself, taking in the fresh air. She now had a good feeling about coming home — hopefully something great would happen during her stay. If not for any other reason, at least connecting with her family.

Brent shook his head. "I can't believe you're home." He swung open the driver's door to his BMW.

"Yeah, me too," Sofia responded while she placed her luggage in the back seat. Brent hadn't changed in some ways. He'd never believed in "ladies first," or had never been the kind of guy to hold a door for a lady. He believed that stuff was overrated. He felt since ladies had equal rights in the workplace, they should be subject to the same expectations as men. And he applied that rule to every circumstance.

***

Once on the road, Sofia made small talk with her brother until they settled into a comfortable silence. She leaned back in her seat to enjoy the scenery. As they drove from Colorado Springs Airport, she watched the mountains over the horizon. Eron was another two hours away, and Sofia was looking forward to the long scenic ride home. Most people didn't like being cooped up in a car for so long, but Sofia always found long rides to be relaxing — even more so when the view was so stunning.

"So, you know," Brent said, breaking the silence, "I finally have a girlfriend."

She turned her gaze away from the majestic mountains scenery and focused on him. "Oh, that's great! What's her name?"

Brent had a wide grin like he was very pleased with himself. "Her name's Mallory … Mallory Baines."

Sofia remained silent, contemplating whether to give Brent an assessment quiz about Mallory. This would give Sofia an idea as to whether Mallory was another snob or a normal down to earth kind of girl. She decided against it and gave a subtle nod instead.

Brent gave her a puzzled look—he had obviously been expecting a different response. After a moment, he asked, "Remember Mr. Baines?"

Sofia frowned, trying to remember, but she couldn't remember anyone named Baines. Still, she didn't miss the excitement in her brother's voice. A small sense of guilt washed over her. But then again, she barely remembered anyone from her elementary or middle school. Most of it had been a blur. Attending a commuter school had made it difficult to keep in touch with friends who lived in a different neighborhood from hers.

"Not really. How long have you two been dating?" Sofia asked

"It's been almost two years." Brent's eyes returned to Sofia. "She's awesome!"

Brent continued talking about his blossoming relationship with Mallory, and what a sweet person she was. Even better, he claimed that everyone in the family, especially their mother, loved her. That was all the information Sofia needed to tell her that Mallory wasn't as sweet as Brent thought she was. Of course, she would be by Brent's standards, but for their mother to like Mallory, the girl was probably as much of an intolerant person as the matriarch of the family. Sofia assumed that would work well for all of them.

She smiled in support of Brent's excitement. However, once Brent was done enthusing about his love life, he directed his attention toward her and asked the question she'd been avoiding. "So, how about you? Any special someone in your life?"

Sofia's smile faded, and she felt uncomfortable at the dreaded question. There was no special someone. She hadn't been successful in finding love, at least not according to her standard.

She shrugged. "I'm not really at that place in my life right now," she responded half-heartedly.

Brent glanced at her and chuckled. "Really? You're twenty-five. What place are you at?"

"I'm still trying to make a name for myself in my career. I don't need the distraction of a relationship." Sofia knew she was just making excuses, although it wasn't really a lie — she was indeed trying to make a name for herself, but so invested was she in that, she often forgot that she needed a little affection in her life.

Brent laughed at her response like it was supposed to be funny, causing Sofia to give him a sharp glare which relayed her displeasure at being laughed at.

"Is that what you plan to tell Mother? She's already planning to fix you up with any of her friends' sons who are eligible bachelors." Brent smiled, clearly amused at his sister's uneasiness. She'd never enjoyed her mother's involvement in her life. His eyes briefly turned from the road to Sofia. "She was making dinner plans with Mr. Velasco, since his son just got divorced."

Sofia rolled her eyes. The thought of her mother clawing her way into her personal life made her stomach churn. Of course, that could never be discounted. Her mother was bound to meddle in her affairs. Sofia had known it was coming before she even got there, and she was fully prepared for the strenuous task of going through multiple dates with all of the snobby sons of her mother's country club friends. It felt as if she was living in olden times, where her mother was desperately trying to marry her off. Sofia cringed at the thought of dating Mr. Velasco's son. Oh, how she needed to psyche herself up for that horror.

Ever since Sofia had turned twelve, her mom had constantly told her what kind of person she was going to marry. Sofia thought that it was absolutely ridiculous. "She can ask, but she won't make me do something I don't want to," Sofia replied with more confidence than she felt on the inside.

Brent gave a disbelieving smirk. "That's going to be very interesting to watch."

They drove along a narrow, curvy highway leading to Eron. The town hadn't changed much, except for a few buildings along Main Street that had been renovated. The rest of the buildings had been white at one time, but the paint was peeling, giving them a salt and pepper appearance. They were definitely in need of a paint job.

Every now and then people waved at them as they drove past. Sofia didn't recognize any of them and doubted Brent did either, but that was merely how people were in small towns.

She was impressed with the friendliness that she had forgotten. In a way, it was as if she was experiencing a small amount of culture shock. Her time away from home had thrown her into places where people, although not explicitly rude, weren't as kind, so that she'd forgotten small town people were more open and friendly.

She spotted the local grocery store where most of the town's people did their shopping. She watched as people strolled in and out of the store. Her gaze moved to the various shops along Main Street that she wasn't too familiar with. Some of them looked intriguing, and she hoped to have time to check them out during her visit. Baskets of vibrant flowers hung by the store entrances, wooden signs declared handmade goods, and there were smiles all around. It was like a whole different world.

As Brent turned onto a familiar road leading home, Sofia's heart raced with mixed emotions, and she was torn between wanting to be back and running away. She stared out the window, letting the lush, green vegetation soothe her. The air smelled fresh, with a hint of pine, and the mountains vibrated with life. The majestic rocks reached up to an endless blue sky, providing Sofia with a beautiful view until Brent took that last turn onto Pleasant Rock Drive.

As Sofia watched the road to home unfold around her, a sudden urge to recapture the magic of her childhood overtook her. She wanted to go back to the time before Eron had closed in around her like a prison. She wanted to go back to those endless summer afternoons with her grandmother, when they'd sat on the deck until sunset, sipping tea from the floral teacups that grandma and grandpa had received as a wedding present from one of their friends. The stories grandma shared of her own childhood delighted Sofia as they giggled about day-to-day stuff.

They pulled into the driveway of Sofia's childhood home. There were two other sedans parked in the driveway, and Brent parked his car behind another sedan.

Sofia remained seated in the car long after Brent had exited. Her stomach in knots, she suddenly felt unsure of her visit home. Was this a good idea? The isolated village she had been in seemed like a sanctuary compared to the tall, elaborate house filled with its own demons. Memories of the past flooded her and her hands began to shake. But it wasn't her mother and the way she would impose on her personal life that frightened her. No, it was far worse than that. It was the thought of seeing her father that left her nervous about stepping out of the car. *I'm here for my grandmother,* she told herself, trying to muster up enough courage to head inside.

Brent had told her all about how her father had regularly read her website for the realtor company she worked for, and how proud he was of her, but the man had never put a phone call through to inform her that he was indeed proud of her. She couldn't help but imagine he was still filled with disappointment at her choices. This would be their first interaction since she'd told him six years ago she wasn't going to work for the family business. And that had ended in a heated argument, thus their silent treatment to each other.

Her door swung open, and she looked up to see Brent standing over her. "Come on out, Sofia. The longer you stay in here, the longer you extend judgment day. You're still going to see him anyway," he said as if he'd read her mind. "I always resented that father liked you more than me, but even I'm ready for you two to reconcile."

Sofia doubted that she was her father's favorite, but didn't feel like arguing with her brother —at least not at the moment when she had bigger fish to fry.

"Whatever happens between you and Father, I am glad you're home," her brother said genuinely.

"Thanks," Sofia said before exiting the car.

"Can you please help me with the big luggage?" She had to ask Brent—otherwise he wouldn't have offered and she would be left hauling both bags on her own.

Brent acquiesced, retrieving Sofia's bag from the back of the car. Sofia carried her small luggage and handbag as she followed Brent in the house. Her heart pounded with each step toward the double doors that led to her childhood home.

CHAPTER 3

Trevor had been busy all morning handling several calls. He'd broken up a fight at the grocery store, and then helped deliver a baby in one of the residential homes in Eron. The lady's husband had gone to work and had taken the only car they had. The woman lived far out of town, and by the time Trevor got to her house, it was too late to make the drive back to the hospital. It wasn't a typical day for most detectives, but since the town was so small, Trevor had to take on whatever jobs police officers normally did during his shift.

After dropping off the new mom and the baby at the hospital, Trevor stopped at home for a brief shower and change of clothing.

When he rummaged through the fridge and couldn't come up with anything to eat, he realized he would need to make a stop at the grocery store on his way back from work. For now, a calzone from Ricci's sounded good; he'd earned himself a meal after the busy morning he'd had.

After turning on his engine, Trevor watched the town behind him disappear as the rolling hills came into view. No matter what time of day or what season, Eron was always beautiful.

He finally approached Main Street, which was lined with a row of shops. There was a Victorian building that housed Eron hotel, a strip of shops and boutiques, an ice cream parlor, and then there was Ricci's. That was where Trevor pulled in and parked.

Just as he was about to exit the car, his radio crackled, and a female voice spoke.

"Hey, Trev." It was Ruth in dispatch, the volunteer who stayed at the police station and answered calls on a part-time basis.

"What's up, Ruth?" Trevor asked.

"The alarm at the Wise Residence has been set off," the voice on the other end explained. Hanging up,

Trevor mumbled under his breath, regretting that he hadn't eaten a granola bar when he'd stopped at home. Now he was starving, but his appetite would have to wait.

Being in a town of almost six thousand people, Eron's police department was horrendously understaffed.

Eron had launched its first police department seven years ago. It'd been perfect timing for Trevor to work there since he'd just graduated from the police academy. He and Scott, their chief, who was retired and in his late fifties, were the first law enforcement officers in Eron until two years ago. The town's people had raised more money for the police department, which had enabled them to hire Enrique Bruno, who worked alongside Trevor and Scott.

Although Trevor was a detective, he still did traffic patrol. The three of them had agreed to take turns, committing to a shift at a time so that they could each have a break. One worked day shifts, the other a night shift and so forth.

The town seemed to need them twenty-four seven for more than criminal cases. They could be called on to do anything from delivering a horse, to directing construction, mediating family disputes, roadside assistance and more.

His hands gripped the steering wheel as he waited for the deer that were crossing the road in front of him. He made his way through the town he loved, going as fast as possible in his SUV, with sirens blaring. He had no time to appreciate the rugged mountains or the meadow to his right as he drove past.

He swerved through the winding road to the high-end part of town called the Rolling Hills and turned onto Pleasant Drive. His car came to a halt in front of the Wise residence. The house was a mansion, especially compared to the homes closer to town. It had one of the best views of the rolling hills that peaked and fell across the vast expanse between the outskirts of town—no wonder this area was called Rolling Hills. He wished he had time to admire the beauty surrounding him, but that was not why he was here.

Trevor had become accustomed to stopping by for false alarms for most residents, but he'd come more often for the Wise family than most. All the times he'd been here before, nothing like a robbery had ever occurred. They needed to speak with their security system provider, he thought. The false alarms were a waste of time, but he didn't mind the welcomed intrusion.

He needed to confirm what he already knew. But it also gave him an opportunity to see the Wises, as a constant reminder that he was still on their back. It also gave him a little twisted joy to see them unnerved whenever they saw him. He figured at least he was keeping them constantly on their toes.

There was no way he would be going through sleepless nights and let the Wise family members be having fun. He needed them agitated, perhaps leading to their confession as to his mother's whereabouts.

As he walked up the cobblestone driveway, there were three sedans parked. He recognized Brent's BMW. Trevor gave the bushes along the side a cursory glance but didn't see anyone. He figured that was a good sign that there hadn't been an actual emergency, unless someone had locked the entire family up in a room somewhere, which seemed unlikely so early in the day, in a residential mountain home. As far as he knew, he was their only enemy.

He scanned the place one more time, keeping one hand close to the gun on his hip, so he could be ready in case he needed to use it. He doubted that he'd have to fire it, but one could never be too careful, especially when he didn't have backup.

He rang the doorbell as soon as he reached the main entrance.

A few seconds later, their chef, Louis, opened the double doors for him. The older man had a large smile on his face, but the smile flitted away once he saw Trevor.

"Detective Freeman," he addressed Trevor formally. Louis had worked with his mother at the Wise mansion, and he had also been vital to the investigations over the years since he knew the ins and outs of the family. While Louis was very loyal to the Wise family, Trevor respected that he didn't let it cloud his sense of judgment. The old man wasn't particularly on his side, because he kept trying to convince Trevor that the Wise family had nothing to do with his mother's disappearance, but he didn't abhor his presence the way the rest of the family did.

"Good afternoon, Louis," Trevor greeted, then added reluctantly. "I'm here because the fire alarm went off." Being a small town, both false and none false alarm calls got kicked over to the police. He already had a feeling that it was a false alarm, since everything seemed to be in order at the Wise home.

Louis cleared his throat. "They were installing the new alarm system, but Mrs. Wise is in the living room." He gestured toward the spacious living area that Trevor could see from the entrance, since it was adjoined to the kitchen.

Louis' face filled with doubt as he debated whether to let Trevor in. That was a rarity. This was the first time he had hesitated in allowing him through, and Trevor couldn't help but suspect that he was interrupting something.

Trevor cocked his brow. "Am I interrupting something?" He was only asking out of courtesy, really—they both knew Trevor Freeman wasn't one to be turned away so easily.

Louis opened his mouth as if to say something, then seemed to change his mind. "Uh … uh. Not really. Come in, son." He stepped aside from the door and allowed Trevor to enter.

Trevor nodded his appreciation to the older man as he walked in, allowing Louis to lead the way, following him further to the sunroom just beyond the living room. He'd visited a few times when his mom worked here, so he knew what each room was.

He could hear sounds of excited chatter and laughter. *Did they have a guest?* he wondered to himself. It was very rare for them to have a party or gathering during the day in the middle of the week, but that was none of his business, although he was quite curious as to who could be visiting the Wises at this hour.

The chatter and laughter died down once the family noticed their unwanted guest. However, one member of the family didn't seem to recognize the change in the mood. Her sonorous laughter lingered when the others had died down, ricocheting off the walls and pulling Trevor's attention to her. Her laughter finally died down as their gazes locked and he watched the humor recede from her features. This was an unfamiliar face—an incredibly beautiful one.

For a moment, he lost track of why he was in their house and what he'd planned to say as his eyes lingered on her. She was the most casually dressed person in the entire room, but her aura was far more magnetic. Her face was free of make-up, allowing him a greater appreciation of her features, like those beautiful green eyes, her small nose, her face round with well-defined brows, her head crowned with blonde hair. And her smile, oh my word! All of which served to make her even more attractive to his eyes. She couldn't be taller than five-foot-four, quite short in comparison to his own height of six-foot-three.

He was still staring at the beauty seated amidst the sea of wolves when one of the wolves got to his feet.

Brent Wise, with a guarded expression, stood directly in front of the female Trevor had been all but ogling, blocking his view of her. "What are you doing here?" he spat out derisively.

Trevor focused unwilling eyes on Brent in a glare. He was in no mood for an argument when he had more important things to do like staring at their guest, perhaps. Unfortunately, Brent had just interrupted his view of such a lovely sight.

Trevor crossed his arms over his chest. "I'm here for the alarm that went off," he replied casually, as he wasn't the slightest bit intimidated by Brent. If it came down to a fight, he could easily take him down, since his job required serious workouts to keep him in shape, but he wasn't here for putting anybody down. "Apparently, I'm not needed after all."

"We're having a new security system installed, and we were testing to see if it works. Didn't Louis tell you before you walked in?" Brent's brows furrowed. "Let's see—"

"It's common protocol, Brent—we get a call, we have to show up." Trevor worked hard at keeping his jaw unclenched. He hoped his face didn't give any of his frustrations away. He straightened himself for better posture in hopes to maintain a calm and confident appearance, yet all he wanted to do was growl at Brent. He could be eating his lunch, but instead, these guys were messing around with alarms and getting mad at him when he did his job. "Something I should have known before I drove this far." His brows lifted. "Next time you should let us know when you mess around with the alarms."

Trevor's eyes strayed once again to the lady. While Brent had slightly blocked his view of her, the five-foot-eleven man wasn't tall enough to entirely prevent it. He could still see her over Brent's head, but not as well as he would have liked. She still had her eyes on him, causing a rush of confidence and curiosity to surge through him.

"Detective Freeman," Marissa Wise spoke as she walked toward him. The woman wore more makeup than Trevor had ever seen in his entire lifetime. She explained to Trevor what Louis and Brent had already told him about them installing a new alarm system. "We are in the middle of a family gathering so we would appreciate it if you kept your visit brief."

Trevor looked over at Marissa, his blood boiling. Who was she kidding? He didn't want to stay any longer than necessary, except for the fact that his eyes kept straying to their guest.

She really had some nerve lecturing him about family gatherings. "Family gathering, huh? We haven't had one of those since my mother disappeared from this house," he reminded her with slight sarcasm.

"And we reiterate that we had nothing to do with that," Brent scolded. "Now, if you'll excuse us, stop interrupting our time and allow the court to settle this, if and when they get enough evidence." Brent's tone was sharp and rising with anger. "You keep showing up on our premises, and we will have to take our concerns to the police department. After all, since when did detectives start investigating false alarms?"

Good luck with calling the police, Trevor thought; since he was the only police on duty at the moment. Not that Scott or Enrique would cuff Trevor for no reason.

"Be that as it may, you already see nothing is happening here. Please see yourself out."

Trevor considered Brent's words without expression. He was tempted to make some remarks of his own, but seeing that they were having a reunion of sorts, he supposed he would hold back on it, if for no one else, for the unassuming beauty who still had her eyes on him. "Of course," he replied dryly. He took one last glance at the mystery lady, then turned around, walking out of the house with an image of her ingrained in his memory.

CHAPTER 4

The next morning, Sofia made her way to the kitchen, where the smell of coffee, syrup, and sausage filled her nostrils.

"Good morning, Louis," she greeted their chef, who did more work for her family than just cooking.

Louis' face lit up. "Miss Wise." He took a step closer and greeted Sofia with a genuine smile that seemed to come naturally to him. The older man had been working for the Wise family since her father was a teenager. Louis had put in over sixty years of service to the family and didn't look like he was retiring anytime soon. Despite his once dark hair being replaced by gray hair, he'd added only a few pounds to his sturdy posture.

Sofia smiled, glad to have at least one transparent person at home.

"Louis." She wrapped her arms around the old man. He was another person she'd greatly missed over the years.

He patted her back lovingly. "I've missed you, Miss Wise," his deep voice rumbled.

"I've missed you too."

Stepping away from the embrace, Louis hung the kitchen towel on the open bar before pulling out the plates.

"I will help myself, thanks, Louis," Sofia said. She didn't need to be served after Louis had already done the cooking.

As soon as she'd taken the first bite of her omelet, her dad, Jason, joined her at the table wearing his sweats and a T-shirt. When he pulled a chair out, Sofia's stomach tied in knots, and her appetite disappeared. What was she going to talk to him about?

She'd seen him briefly last night, and all she'd managed was a hello. Her dad had only nodded and said he was glad she was home. So much for connecting with her family over this visit! She took a deep breath, accepting the fact that this was going to be a long two months.

"Good morning," her dad greeted, his green eyes giving nothing away. He sat and poured himself a glass of orange juice from the pitcher that Louis had placed on the table.

"Hello, Father." She forced a smile as she struggled with an inner battle for her next words. She couldn't think of what to say next.

At least it was a start at communication. Sofia was to blame for the most part because she'd always been the kid who gave her parents a run for their money. Always arguing and doing the opposite of what they wanted. At fifteen, she'd requested to move to New York to live with her aunt. Thankfully, both parents had been on board with it.

They ate breakfast in awkward silence until she rose from her seat with a half-eaten omelet on the plate in her hand. Louis' breakfast buffet would have to wait for later. Perhaps she would return for the pancakes and sausage, so she could enjoy them in silence.

"I'm going golfing this afternoon at the country club," her dad said to her back. She turned to face him. "I would like for you to join me if you don't have plans."

Was that his way of trying to reconcile?

She winced. "I ... actually have plans. Maybe next time."

Jason didn't press the issue, just turned his gaze back to his plate.

The rest of the day, Sofia spent settling in and visiting with her mom, which let Sofia know that Marissa's personality hadn't changed much. It surprised Sofia that her mom, a woman who'd never worked in her life, still kept money and wealth as the main topics of her conversations.

Sofia put up with the money talk until her mom's conversation shifted to eligible bachelors that would suit Sofia's status.

"Tobin Velasco has agreed to come to dinner tonight," Marissa spoke enthusiastically. Whoever Tobin was, Sofia had no interest in finding out. She shifted her head to face her mom, who sat inches away from her on the sofa.

"Glad you're having some friends over, Mom."

Marissa placed her hand over Sofia's. The middle-aged woman looked like she had barely aged a day since Sofia had last seen her. They'd kept in touch once every three months. "No, darling, I would like to introduce him to you, he's now single. Did you know that he's one of the wealthiest young men in El Paso County?"

"Mom." Sofia's hands went up in exasperation. "I don't need you to set up my dates." Perhaps hanging out with her dad would be better than her pretending to enjoy a visit with some guy. "Actually, I do have plans this afternoon."

Marissa's mouth dropped open and then shut.

"I'm golfing with Dad," Sofia said.

"Your brother wants you to meet Mallory."

"I will meet Mallory and leave immediately, how about that?"

Marissa's shoulders sagged. "But …" She was already marching out of the room, letting the rest of her mom's words bounce right off her back.

Jason Wise seemed excited that Sofia had changed her mind about going golfing with him. He'd left two hours earlier and told Sofia he was going to make sure everything was ready for her when she showed up at the country club.

As Sofia stepped out from her bedroom with a backpack strapped to her back, the click of high heels and excited chatter echoing down the hall announced that they had a guest.

"Oh, my sweet, darling girl," Marissa was saying with enthusiasm as Sofia stepped into the living room to see her mom with a lady standing a few feet away from her.

Marissa pulled Sofia into a hug. It didn't feel quite as warm as Louis' had felt, but her mother wasn't one who gave out a lot of hugs. Sofia assumed she should take this with a smile. Granted, her mother wasn't the warmest of people and hadn't been the best mom, but flaws and all, Sofia found she really enjoyed the brief embrace.

The lady stood aside, watching the exchange between Sofia and Marissa, a tiny smile on her lips. She looked like a mini-Marissa. They were both dressed similarly, the only difference being that the younger lady's hair was in a ponytail. Sofia didn't doubt that this new entrant was Mallory, her brother's girlfriend. It would make sense that her mother was already grooming her into the perfect wife.

"This is Mallory," Marissa introduced the brunette who mirrored her own mannerisms. "Mallory, darling, this is my daughter, Sofia."

Mallory flashed a rehearsed smile, but Sofia supposed a girl modeled after her mother would happen to have one of those smiles.

"It's so nice to meet you, Sofia. I've heard so much about you." Mallory spoke in a sugary sweet voice. *Yup, just like Mother,* Sofia thought.

Sofia smiled. "Good things, I hope," she said as she turned her gaze toward Marissa, who nodded in agreement.

"I'm sorry I have to run, but it was nice to meet you, Mallory." Sofia shook hands with their guest.

"You need to wait and say hello to Tobin at least," Marissa said.

Sofia's brows shot up. "Seriously, Mother?" She turned to make her exit, leaving Marissa and her guest standing speechless.

**

The past three days spent at home had felt more constructive than Sofia had thought they would be. Just as she'd resigned herself to hopelessness, her father had started making more of an effort to reconnect with her. Though there wasn't much to talk about without triggering any potential arguments, they'd managed to hold a few short conversations. He still seemed reserved around her, but she and the old man were bonding in their own way.

After golfing, they'd shared dinner at the country club. Jason still attempted to question Sofia about why she wasn't interested in working for the family business, but Sofia had shifted the conversation away from business to personal conversations. Golfing with her dad had turned out better then she'd expected.

She still couldn't believe her mother had invited Tobin Velasco over, trying to set the two of them up. The poor man had wasted his time.

As everything fell into place, and she realized her visit back home wasn't quite as taxing as she'd thought it was going to be, she turned her attention to one more item of business she needed to figure out— why couldn't she stop thinking about the handsome dark detective that had stopped by? The man was built like he was very familiar with a gym or physical labor. It wasn't just about his connection to her family and what he was potentially accusing them of, but she felt intrigued by the man himself. His visit on the day she'd arrived had left everyone uneasy, but no one wanted to give her details. A reminder of how her parents still treated her like a teenager.

Brent had always been their puppet, doing whatever it took to earn approval from their parents, and Sofia had always been the opposite, perhaps reason enough for her family to keep her in the dark on their schemes. Why would anything be different this time? She had thought her visit would change things. She'd missed her family, and needed to reconnect, or at least something close to that, and what better place than the quiet town she'd grown up in?

Now she was starting to think that wouldn't be happening, and instead she would be thrown into another of her family's controversy.

Sofia opened the blinds to the huge glass window in her bedroom—her childhood room, except the pink color she'd grown up with on the wall had been replaced by a neutral tan. Memories still flooded her each time she came into this room. She remembered the endless nights of playing with her own dolls, although her dollhouse was long gone. Her eyes went to the view of the Rocky Mountains. The rays of the colorful sunset shooting above them pumped up her adrenaline to do something more than stay within the walls of the mansion. She had never appreciated the view in all the time growing up here, and yet now, she finally realized how much she'd missed it.

She'd gone for a run earlier and discovered several trails that she planned to check out over the next few days, but now, the sunset above the mountains and the few rolling hills from her view were tantalizing, and the last three hours she'd been in the house were enough for a city girl from New York, where life was like a highway. She had already had her fill of peace and quiet for the day.

Things were somehow still the same as they'd always been in the Wise residence, where everybody ate meals whenever they felt like, at their own pace. There was no teamwork to anything. They had all reverted to the cold demeanor she had almost been convinced had gone extinct after spending a day with them. So much for that.

There was a town she needed to explore, and not the country clubs, where the wealthy people went. She wanted to check out the rest of Eron where regular people went. The memory of the country store and the smells of the natural soaps came to mind. The last time she'd been to that store, she'd only been twelve, and her friend Chloe Love had taken her there. Her mom had been upset when she found out Sofia had gone shopping in a local store and had ordered her to never go back there again. Even in New York, each time she missed Eron, the country store seemed to come to mind. Now that she was older, she could drive herself anywhere and shop at any store she wanted, with her own money.

There were three cars sitting in the garage—one of them was her grandma's, which meant it was basically hers now. She still knew how to navigate her way through the town, and needed to breathe in the fresh mountain air and perhaps meet other people besides her own family members.

She threw on a pair of shorts and a floral tank top, slipped on strappy sandals, and made her way out of her room.

No sooner had she twisted the garage doorknob than her father's deep voice rang from the stairs, stopping her movement. "And where exactly are you going?"

She looked up towards the staircase and found her father at the top of it, looking down on her. Just because she'd gone golfing with him didn't mean things had gone back to her teenage years when he could boss her around.

"To the country store."

"Why? The house is stocked with everything you need. You must have forgotten that we don't shop there," he said in a flat tone.

Trying to ignore the reminder that her family didn't shop in the small country store, Sofia winced. "Actually, I don't think you have everything I need in this house."

Her dad proceeded to list all the reasons as to why she shouldn't be mingling with the locals, and how convenient it would be if she'd shop online instead.

Sofia rolled her eyes. Again with the controlling, she thought.

"I don't want anything to be picked out for me, and I don't want to shop online." That was all she did in the big city. "I want to go meet some locals in Eron."

She figured the country store would be a start. She'd gone to some private elementary school fifteen miles away from Eron. She and her brother had a driver who took them every day. She doubted she would see any of her former schoolmates in the town unless she went to the country club.

"You could meet people at the country club," Jason said. The club belonged to the Wises, of course.

Sofia sighed. "I want to go out, Dad, and not to the country club. I want to talk to other people who don't choose their words in my presence."

"You won't be as welcome there as you'd think." His tone was more serious than she'd expected.

She drew her head back in surprise. "Really, Dad? How many people have you guys offended since I left? I mean, aside from that detective guy."

Her father's expression grew cold at the mention of the detective. Sofia had tried not bringing him up since that day, mostly because when she had asked about him, they had told her it was nothing she

61

needed to worry her head over, and nobody seemed willing to divulge anything of importance to her. She assumed the detective had hit her family's nerves somehow, but she also hadn't mentioned him because she had been trying to forget about the man, and mentioning him meant bringing back memories of him. She wasn't sure why, but his face had filled her mind, and she hoped to see him again.

While the detective's presence in the house had been quite brief, Sofia swore it had been the longest five minutes of her life. As soon as her eyes had fallen on the dark-skinned man, her gaze didn't seem to wander to anything else but the guy, and while she would like to say that connection had nothing to do with his height, powerful build, handsome face or deep, soothing voice, she knew that played just as much a part as the sheer power and authority dripping off him. The man had controlled the conversation in the room, and he had walked into their house, spread discomfort all around, and walked out with a confidence that was awe-inspiring. Sofia had never known any of her family members to be so meek in the presence of anyone else, and it left her wondering what exactly the man had on them.

"You shouldn't pry into things you have no business meddling with, Sofia. And it would be best if you weren't running around this town without being properly informed," he said coldly.

Sofia frowned. "The whole family seems to have some business with this man, and my family's business is my business." Since you guys won't tell me a thing, maybe the town's people will be more forthcoming with information. " I'll see you later, Dad."

She didn't waste an extra second looking at her father or listening to whatever protests he was coming up with—she turned and walked towards the garage, leaving her dad standing there with his mouth open.

She assumed the store owner knew everything that went on in Eron. She didn't exactly know him well, but she remembered that he'd been friendly enough for her friend Chloe to make jokes with. She wondered if people would remember her. What would they think of a Wise meandering about downtown?

CHAPTER 5

Staring at several similar items in his hands, Trevor crinkled up his face in a mix of annoyance and confusion. He hated shopping for tampons. Not only did he find buying them demeaning, he also found the exercise uncomfortable and far more difficult than any stings he'd ever been on in his investigations. He dreaded the times Keisha called and requested him to pick up tampons on his way back home.

It didn't matter how many times he'd done this. Trevor could say confidently that each time he went to the feminine hygiene aisle people looked at him funny. With it being a small town, word got out fast on the street about how the town detective shopped for tampons for his sister. Still, it never got any easier, and to make matters worse, he never quite remembered which brand she'd asked for, despite having bought the same brand on multiple occasions. He told himself it was because it was just too traumatizing to remember.

He reached for the phone in his pocket to call her. Shaking his head, he shoved his phone back when he thought of anybody eavesdropping on his conversation regarding tampons. He knew it was a bit foolish to be this worked up, but he couldn't help it.

He couldn't wait for her to get a car so that Trevor would not have to run her errands anymore, which was going to take a long time since she was taking online college classes. Trevor hoped by next year they would have raised enough money to buy a second-hand car, and Keisha would have a decent job to pay for gas and insurance.

Instead of calling her, he decided to stand there and try to figure out which tampons were which. Why did everything about girls have to be so complicated? Even worse, how did he end up in this predicament? Why did they make so many brands, and what was the difference between daytime, nighttime, light, and thick?

Sighing in frustration, he looked from one package to the other. If he couldn't make up his mind, he would grab any of them and let Keisha deal with whatever objections she had. That would teach her to plan ahead, so he could get her into town to buy her own feminine products.

"You should go for the one in your right hand." A soft, feminine voice came from his left.

He'd been completely unaware that he had an audience. *Great, just great!* Humiliated, he looked up, only to find none other than the lady he had seen at the Wise residence. She was standing within reach from him, a beautiful smile on her face.

Trevor could only stare at her, his words suddenly failing him for some inexplicable reason. Close up, she was a stunning sight to behold. There was an unexpected warmth about her that defied the natural coldness that came with being part of the Wise family. It was hard to believe she was one of them. He had yet to find out the exact relationship she shared with them, but considering the similar features between her and the patriarch of the family, the uncomfortable knot in his stomach told him she was one of them.

Wasn't Brent supposed to have a sister that had gone away for a period of time? His mother had mentioned that the Wises had a daughter somewhere out of state. Could it be that this was her?

"It's much better, you can take my word for it," she added, that bright smile still lighting up her face.

It took him half a second to realize she was talking about the packages of tampons in his hands, "Oh ... oh! I ... thank you." He chuckled nervously as he returned the package in his left hand to the shelf, hoping her recommendation was the correct one. Of all the places to run into her, it had to be in the ladies' sanitary section of the grocery store. He had thought for sure if he saw her again, it would be in a far more dignifying setting, not here, holding tampon boxes.

"You're welcome," she replied, then teased. "So, who's the lucky girl that has you buying tampons?"

He smiled at her question. If only Keisha knew just how lucky she was. "It's for my sister," he responded.

"Lucky her. My brother won't even touch my shoes. Meanwhile, someone out there has a brother getting tampons for her. I hope she's highly appreciative of your efforts."

Trevor smiled. She certainly made the act seem far more noble than he thought it was. He was getting tampons for Keisha—lots of guys made tampon runs all over the United States ... right? It wasn't like he had a choice. As a matter of fact, he begrudged completing his sister's request.

"Well, forgive me for saying so, but your brother must be ..." his voice trailed off, thinking of a term to describe Brent, assuming he was her brother. Then he realized it probably wasn't a great idea to insult the possible brother of the beautiful woman in front of him. "I don't know what to say, but he's different, let's just say that."

She grinned at him, showing off an impressive set of pearly whites. "I couldn't agree more," she stated, causing a smile to spring upon his face. She stretched out her hand to him.

"The name's Sofia. I understand my last name leaves a sour taste in your mouth, so I'll just let you figure it out yourself."

Oh, he had figured it out all right. Sofia Wise. While her surname did indeed set off warning bells in his head, Trevor found the bearer quite pleasant. She was nothing like the rest of her family—at least she didn't act like it. Her calm and friendly demeanor seemed to prove she didn't have a bad bone in her, but even more, he got the feeling that she knew who he was and the relationship he had with her family. Yet it hadn't stopped her from talking to him. And to Trevor, that said more about her and the type of person she was than anything else. Unless, of course, she was being manipulative—but something in his gut told him that wasn't the case. Her eyes were too sincere as she continued to hold out her hand.

He reached out and enveloped her tiny hand in his larger one. "I'm Trevor. I understand my surname leaves a shiver in the bodies of your family members, so I'll just let you figure it out yourself," he responded, paraphrasing her own words.

"It's nice to meet you, Trevor."

"It's nice to meet you, too, Sofia," he replied.

Trevor had never felt more clueless than in that moment. What was he doing standing here and talking to someone from the Wise family? That family was filled with the scum of the earth—they were the source of his sleepless nights.

Doubts filled his mind again. What were the chances that they hadn't set their daughter on him to find his weakness or infiltrate his non-existent love life until she was able to convince him to stop the investigations into his mother's case? Could he trust her? Trevor knew that when Sofia's mom wanted something, she would get it regardless of the cost. If Marissa had wanted someone's salon, before anybody knew it, the Wises had paid it off and owned it. They'd blackmailed people who owned it into selling their land to them.

So many possibilities hovered in the recesses of Trevor's mind, but he could only focus on this pretty lady with an angelic smile and an infectious charm. He would deal with the inevitable repercussions of his actions later. Besides, it wasn't as if he was divulging the secrets of his case against her family—and no one would stop him from investigating his mother's disappearance. He had made a pact with himself long ago that he'd search for his mother until the day he died. It had become his main focus in life.

He knew it wasn't healthy, though. He should put his attention on the Lord, but he couldn't seem to let go of this part of his life. This missing hole that seemed to engulf his entire being. He figured God would understand. He'd lost his mother. He had to seek justice for her—besides, wasn't God adamant about justice, anyway?

Still, when he walked away, his mind wasn't dwelling on what Sofia might be hiding. It was reliving the moment of holding her hand and the way her eyes seemed to fill something inside him—and that terrified him.

CHAPTER 6

Trevor ran in the mornings. It woke him up, kept him in shape, and gave him time to think and to praise God. It was a welcome change from his usual thoughts—he thought about his mom and wondered how to come down to the end of the case. When his mind wasn't consumed by that, he found himself thinking about his work, or more recently, like today, it was Sofia on his mind.

He preferred thinking about Sofia, though he knew he shouldn't. He was playing with a fire he was sure was going to burn him, but he couldn't stop himself. He even prayed about it as he ran. With each silent word, begging God to let him know if he could trust Sofia, he ran faster. Every time he mentioned her in prayer, peace and warmth filled his heart, as if confirming that she was safe—but again, he couldn't be sure, since they'd just met. He just needed his mind to be on the same page of that reality.

The morning was bright with colorful clouds above the horizon and the rows of mountains. Trevor never ceased to be awed by the beauty of Eron. He glanced at his watch just as he heard a voice from behind.

"Hey!"

It was his friend and colleague Enrique, the third staff member at Eron PD.

Night or day, the guy always had his brown hair nicely brushed. Enrique had moved to Eron from Italy six years ago to join his family that owned Ricci's, an Italian restaurant. Despite Enrique's family's desire for him to work full time at the cafe, he'd gone to the police academy and thankfully had been hired with Eron PD. He still worked at Ricci's whenever he was off duty.

It surprised Trevor that Enrique hated running, since that's all his friend had done growing up. He had an athletic body frame, and Trevor knew that the guy could take down just about anything that got in his path. Trevor had seen him do it several times. He'd asked Trevor to be accountable for his running since he needed to keep the pace for his job.

The guy was a one-man wrecking crew when he wanted to be, with a warm presence—a good reason he'd become Trevor's close friend.

"You're late!" Trevor said.

"I'm here, aren't I?" Enrique responded nonchalantly.

They ran silently, along a non- designated raggedy trail and Trevor picked up his speed as they climbed a hill and leaped over a few rocks the further they got.

"Looks like no leisure run today, eh?" Enrique asked, gasping for air between each word. Trevor ignored him, pushing himself to run faster.

"You're running me hard today, bro. What's up with all the military-style training?"

Enrique was always joking, trying to get a rise out of others. He exaggerated his accent when teasing, to be funny.

Trevor was tempted to discuss his encounter with Sofia Wise to someone besides his family. All of his friends knew his relationship with the Wises.

The mountain peaks vibrated with a bright orange and pink sky as Trevor slowed his pace and Enrique caught up to him.

They came to a stop, allowing their breathing to calm before doing a few stretches on the massive rocks in their surroundings.

"Are you going to tell me what's eating you up?" Enrique asked. Trevor had almost forgotten that Enrique always knew when he wasn't himself.

"How's work going at the restaurant?" Trevor asked, completely ignoring the question his buddy had directed to him.

Enrique let out a loud laugh that echoed in the valley below them. "Now you are really being funny." He caught his chest as the laughter subsided. "You're interested in hearing about my parents' restaurant, huh?"

"Yeah, I want to know."

"After you answer my question. What's up with you?"

Trevor shook his head. "There's nothing up, Enrique."

They ran back to the bottom of the trail.

A woman with a tiny figure was jogging toward them. Trevor didn't need to take a second look to know that it was the beautiful blonde woman he'd met a couple of times already. He could swear his heart rate had kicked up, and it had nothing to do with the running itself. He slowed down.

"What's up?" Enrique asked. "You all stiff and frozen." His gaze shifted to the lady ahead. "Wait ... do you know the woman headed this way?"

"Sofia Wise," Trevor spoke, his voice so low that Enrique almost didn't hear.

Enrique gasped. That's when Trevor realized he'd spoken out loud.

"Isn't she—"

"Out of my league, yeah." The words came out without thinking. And yes, Enrique was very aware of Trevor's odd relationship with the Wise family.

"That's not what I was going to say, but—"

Sofia was within earshot before Enrique finished his sentence.

She slowed down as they approached. Her smile was radiant. She sure had a killer smile, enough to melt the person on the receiving end.

She wasn't nearly as sweaty as Trevor and Enrique. Trevor found himself returning her smile without any effort, and so did Enrique, who couldn't hide his curiosity.

"Hi, detective," she spoke breathlessly.

Trevor brushed his hand through his tight black curls. He'd had a haircut recently, but it was messy enough you couldn't tell. Why was he being self-conscious about his hair? This was the last place he would have expected to run into Sofia. Especially up in the mountain trails. She continued to surprise him, and he found himself wanting to know more about her.

The Wises owned a country club that served as their lair. Did her parents know that she was running early this morning where the locals did? Trevor wondered how she'd found out about the trails. Amused, he asked, "You run, too?"

Enrique flashed an amused grin at Sofia, followed by a questioning brow to Trevor.

Sofia put her hand out to Enrique. "I'm Sofia Wise."

Enrique nodded, his grin widening, and Trevor gave him a warning glare.

Clearing his throat, Enrique put out his hand. "Enrique Bruno. Trevor's work partner." He bent and planted a soft kiss on Sofia's hand. If Trevor didn't know Enrique with his charming personality, he might have been jealous of the relaxed way he greeted Sofia.

In an attempt to say something, Trevor asked, "Are you familiar with the trails here?"

"I stumbled on this one when I took a walk two days ago. Are there more trails you would recommend?"

Trevor opened his mouth to respond, but Enrique squeezed his shoulder.

"Yeah, Trevor here is a native and knows all the best trails there's to know. He will help you out." He slapped Trevor on the back. "Restaurant duty is calling." He was off and running before Trevor could respond. *Great!* he thought to himself. Trevor would have to throttle him later.

"Do you have a few minutes to walk with me?" Sofia asked, her green eyes soft as they met Trevor's. He didn't want to mingle with a Wise. Definitely not in his best interest and he knew it, yet … here she was with a bright smile and hopeful eyes.

"Sure," his mouth said without permission from his brain.

Trevor felt his body tighten as he walked silently beside Sofia. He found himself wishing they'd just run, so he didn't have to wonder what to say.

"I don't mind running again if that's what you wish to do," he suggested.

"I would rather walk," she said, and they strolled to a narrower, winding trail perfect for walking.

Trevor felt nervous around her, but he enjoyed her company. If the town's people found out, which they would somehow, they were going to have a field day gossiping about his new lady friend.

"Tell me more about Eron," Sofia said. "Have you always lived here?"

"Yes, my parents were born in the town, and my dad's great-grandparents, and it goes back even farther. Their great-grandparents were ranchers passing through from New Mexico and decided to settle here with their cattle." He gestured to the meadows before them. "As you can see, all the green grass and the creeks around were enough to sustain their animals. Obviously, owning a farm isn't everyone's life goals these days, and there's not a whole lot going on out here in Eron, but I didn't have a reason to leave." His voice lowered when he spoke. "Especially after mom went missing."

She stopped walking. So did Trevor.

Sofia looked up, and his gaze collided with hers. She pressed her soft fingers over his. "I am so sorry you lost your mom," she said sincerely, her eyes expressing genuine concern.

"Hey, Detective!" A female voice made them turn their heads. Since the trail had been vacant when they'd started walking they were both caught off guard. It was Stephanie, a slightly plump woman in her early thirties who ran her parent's ice cream shop. If you wanted the news to travel fast in Eron, Stephanie was the right person to get the word out.

Trevor nodded his greeting, then returned his gaze to their joined hands.

He felt a wave of electricity from Sofia's simple touch, and his body tightened. He moved his fingers out of hers.

Trevor still suspected Sofia's family, based on the last evidence he'd seen of a picture of a man who resembled Jason Wise standing with his mom. The photo had been taken in Utah, according to his friend Dan Reading, who worked as an investigator for missing persons in Colorado Springs. Dan had been helping Trevor in tracing his mom's whereabouts. Because the man in the picture was turned slightly away from the camera, neither Trevor nor Dan could make out his features clearly enough to make a positive ID.

He figured it was best not to talk about his mom. He still wasn't sure of Sofia's intentions, and though her sympathies felt sincere, Trevor didn't want to divulge any more details. It was against the rules of the case, anyway.

"Thanks," he said solemnly, then changed the subject.

Sofia Wise, intriguing as she was, was dangerous to him in more ways than just a distraction to his investigations.

***

It had been almost a week since Sofia's return home. She'd slowly gotten into a routine of sorts. She'd gone jogging and ran into Trevor and Enrique twice besides that first time she'd run into them.

She also worked on her business from home since she'd brought her laptop. Her personal assistant back in New York was still handling the business and clients.

She had avoided the country club altogether, even though she managed to spend one on one time with her family. She'd had brunch with her dad at one of the fancy restaurants. Another opportunity to slowly mend their rocky relationship.

Yesterday, she'd gone out for lunch with her brother, and had been shopping with her mom earlier today.

She now relaxed in a wicker chair on the back porch, giving herself a few minutes to enjoy the afternoon. Their house sat on the rocky hills, offering one of the greatest views of the lush green valley. Sofia assumed her brother liked the view just as much as she did, since most of the times she'd been there he seemed to prefer working on the porch as he answered calls for clients.

Brent worked alongside their dad running multiple hotels the Wises owned in Colorado and a few other states they were expanding into. Besides managing the overall operations and resources of the company, he did most of the marketing, too. Brent was very knowledgeable in investment and profitable ventures.

Brent was also a good business advisor, or at least he used to be. He knew exactly how to help people make a profit, but Sofia assumed if he still did anything like that these days, it was all for the benefit of the Wise Enterprise. Buying any business that failed, instead of saving it.

Brent did most of his work from his home office, only leaving the house when he had to meet with clients, which he did often.

Sofia's phone chimed with an incoming text, and she reached for it from her lap. She hoped it was Trevor, since they'd been texting back and forth for the last hour, but Trevor hadn't responded for the last ten minutes. It was probably the last two minutes, but it seemed like ten to her.

Yep, it was Trevor.

Her heart fluttered at the sight of his name on her phone's screen. She had exchanged numbers with him the first time they'd met on a run.

Enrique had left early both times, which had given Sofia more time with Trevor. Sofia had been pleased to find that he was easy to talk to. They'd rested on a rock beside the jogging trail, and she'd told him about her stay in New York and her purpose of returning to Eron. He had sympathized with her on the loss of her grandmother and offered to help if there were anything he could do.

She had wanted to bring up the case he had with her parents, but she didn't want to risk ruining their already blossoming relationship so soon. She'd boldly asked for Trevor's phone, so she could enter her number into his phone and had sent a text to herself from it to save Trevor's number.

Sofia couldn't shake the feeling that the detective might feel something for her, as well—maybe she just wanted him to feel that way, but she planned to find out soon.

Sofia was aware of her brother's speculative gaze on her. He had been sneaking glances at her for the last hour, and all it served to do was make her exaggerate her actions. She knew he was curious. She had been fiddling with her phone, smiling at the gadget, even, so yes, he was expected to be a wee bit curious about the reason for this.

She laughed at another joke Trevor had cracked through the text, and this time it was enough to move Brent to action. "I wonder who's got you this excited," he began.

She glanced at him. "It's just a friend," she responded casually, her eyes glued to the screen rather than daring to sneak a glance at Brent. Her smile widened as she typed another message to respond to Trevor.

"A friend, really? From New York?" Brent asked with his brows up.

Sofia sighed and rolled her eyes. "How is this any of your business?" she shot at him.

"No need to be so hostile. I'm only trying to protect you."

That was ridiculous, considering Brent didn't particularly care about her protection. She couldn't remember a time in their lives when Brent had actually protected her. Instead, he had thrown her under the bus multiple times—he was definitely not the protective type. "I think you would be put to better use running dad's errands," she said sarcastically.

Brent frowned at her retort; she could tell she had hit a nerve with that. Her brother hadn't really gotten used to leaving their father's wings. Even when Brent had left home and gone to Oxford for his business degree, he still seemed only to do things that favored their father in his career. She wouldn't deny he had made quite the name for himself over the years at Wise enterprise. His pay was mouth-watering, but still, he was quick to do his father's bidding and had yet to really learn what it meant to be his own man.

He got to his feet. "I know who you're chatting with," he said pointedly. Sofia looked over at him and cocked a brow. "I hope for your sake Dad doesn't find out. Or I should say, for his sake."

"Who appointed you to be the moral police around here? In case you hadn't noticed, I've lived on my own for the last ten years. Oh, and we're adults—hello?"

Brent turned and slid open the glass doors that led into the house from the back porch.

Sofia got back to her phone and read Trevor's text.

Would you like to come to church with me tomorrow?

She had to think about that for a moment. Church wasn't as foreign to her since she'd been thinking about it a lot lately, especially after her grandmother's death. Her visit to Africa the week her grandma had died had been an opening factor to what

Eunice had taught her. The seed had been planted, and now the dots were slowly connecting.

Trevor had mentioned they had two services, and that the crowd at the early service was quite small. Which would be better for Sofia, since she was still nervous about all that.

Can we go to the early service if I decide to go?

Her phone chimed a response. *Early service is fine.*

She wanted to go to church, but had no idea if she would fit in.

"Send me the address; I will text you by 6:00 a.m. if I can make it."

After Trevor's final text with the address, Sofia set her phone aside and let out a huff. She had finally met a guy she could talk to—a guy who wasn't an airhead, one who made her laugh, and the best thing was, she didn't have to go to her mother's country club engagements to find him. Brent could yap all he wanted, but Sofia knew she wasn't going to cease communication with Trevor regardless of their differences.

They would all learn that she was an adult, capable of making her own decisions and nobody was going to police her around.

***

Finally caught up on the paperwork that had been piled on his desk, Trevor yawned. He rose from his seat and stretched his arms, letting out another yawn. The morning hadn't been as busy as usual, which gave him an opportunity to go fix Theda's faucet. Theda was a seventy-something-year-old who owned the ice cream shop downtown which was manned by her daughter Stephanie.

Theda always called Trevor whenever she had handiwork that needed to be done. Trevor didn't mind helping her out whenever he had the time. She was one of the faithful people in Eron. She attended all committee meetings, made most of the pies for their fundraisers, and on July 4th, the busiest day for the ice cream shop, fifty percent of the proceeds from the ice cream went to the police department.

"There you are!" the short, stocky lady said as Trevor stepped through her front door. Theda might be seventy-four, but she had the energy of a twenty-year-old. The dusting of flour or powder on her apron matched her fair skin and short white hair.

"Hi, Theda," Trevor greeted, and the lady wrapped her arms around him for a hearty embrace.

"When am I going to meet that girl of yours?" she asked after the embrace.

Trevor chuckled. "There's no girl out there just yet, but you will be the first to know."

Her brows furrowed. "I mean Sofia Wise."

Trevor's jaw dropped. He'd almost forgotten that Theda's daughter had seen him with Sofia. Both Theda and Stephanie loved to gossip. Like mother, like daughter.

Trevor grinned and shook his head. "I better get that faucet of yours looked at."

After drinking the cold glass of lemonade that Theda had forced on him, Trevor finally left her house, carrying a bag of homemade brownies that she'd also insisted he take. He made a quick stop at an auto shop where he needed to do a preliminary investigation on a break-in from the night before.

Achak, the store's Native American owner, had told Trevor to stop by around 11:00 a.m. when he would close the store temporarily for their meeting.

The robbers had taken some of the tools from the shop, but Trevor was positive the tools would be recovered. He noted the pry marks on the back door, which stood open, then scanned the shop's interior for any additional doors. His gaze returned to the pried door, his attention drawn to something that was bothering him about it.

"What makes you think it was a break-in?" Trevor kept his face expressionless as he questioned the tall, thirty-something man.

"Well ..." Achak tugged nervously at his long black ponytail. "The doorknob was pulled out and ..."

"Who else has the keys to the store?" Trevor asked, examining the scratches on the bolt again, careful not to touch anything before he dusted for fingerprints. He stepped back for a better look at the splintered doorframe, then turned back to Achak and pointed to the marred doorknob. "See that? These are pry marks. Someone let themselves in through the front door and then pried this open to make it look like it was broken into from the outside."

Achak mulled the words over for a second before he spoke. "My brother has a key."

Trevor nodded. "I'll need to ask him a few questions."

The break-in had definitely been an inside job. It had either been Achak's brother, or someone else had gotten the keys from the family somehow. This wasn't the first time Trevor had dealt with a theft committed by a family member. He had no doubt he was going to get to the bottom of this case more sooner than later.

The police station was still in the old farmhouse, but they had enough land that they'd build a bigger office once they'd raised enough funds for it.

Back at the station, Trevor narrowed his gaze as he pulled into the dirt parking lot, focused on one of the two cars in the lot. He decided to ignore the unfamiliar sedan and moved towards the building, only to stop short at the sight of a familiar slender figure waiting in one of the three chairs outside the front office.

His eyes took her in as he kept himself from tripping. She was dressed in a floral sundress with green print. Her hair fell over her shoulders and looked beautiful.

His heart leaped with all sorts of emotions he couldn't identify as he called out her name.

"Sofia!"

"Hello, Detective." Sofia rose from the seat, giving him a once over. "It's nice to see you in action." After she had taken him all in, her gaze traveled to his hip, where he'd tucked his gun into his jeans.

She fanned herself with her hand, before reaching into her tote. "I brought some pastries from the town's bakery." She pulled out a small brown bag and handed it to Trevor. "I hope they're good."

Pleased, Trevor smiled and took the bag from her. "Well, thank you. Everything they make in Eron is good."

He gestured to the entrance. "We could go inside, but there's no air conditioning."

"I don't mind sitting here, actually," Sofia said.

Trevor gestured for her to sit and sat on the chair next to her. He then placed the bag on the third chair.

"I'm on a mission to get to know the town, and while I'm at it, I figured why not stop by and surprise you?" She smiled, and her smile did something to Trevor's stomach. He liked seeing her smile.

Trevor didn't mind this kind of surprise at all. "I'm so glad you stopped by. Please feel free to stop by anytime." He couldn't explain the joy he felt at her presence and her company. Although he didn't want to think of her visit being temporary, he needed to know how long he was going to get to enjoy this, whatever it was.

"How long are you in town?"

She shrugged. "I took two months off work, but I could stay longer if I have a reason to do so."

He wished he would be a reason for her to extend her stay. It was a foolish thought, but he couldn't help himself. "Tell me more about New York, and why you stayed away from Eron for so long that I never met you before?"

She ran a hand through her hair. "My parents and I fought often. I spent more time with my grandma, but then I ended up going to live with my aunt in New

York, where I attended high school and started my career." Trevor listened as she talked about her travels to Africa, her desire to connect with family. "I'm so disappointed in my family since their main focus in life is always money and status."

Her gaze was distant as she stared into the open field ahead of them.

Trevor wondered what had triggered a fifteen-year-old to leave her parents. He couldn't imagine his sister Keisha moving far from him.

"What made you decide to move so far from home?"

She took a deep breath. "I hated all the parties my parents hosted each weekend. I just wanted to relax after a busy week of school, but they had all their friends over. They'd drink like crazy. And they had kids who were much older than me, maybe not so much for Brent, so they'd drink, too." Her shoulders tensed and Trevor saw a pained memory in her eyes. Had something bad happened to her? He hoped not, because he would hate to have to lay hands on whoever haunted her memories.

"Anyway, we better eat those pastries," she said, changing the subject.

Trevor knew when not to press someone for details, and he opened the bakery bag.

They both enjoyed the sweet treats, sharing the bottled water she'd brought.

"Tell me about your faith," she asked. "What motivated you to put your faith in God?"

Trevor's gaze went to the water bottle in front of him as he tried to come up with the right response.

After they'd made plans to go to church two days ago, Sofia had texted him with apologies and promised that she would try to come to church the following Sunday.

"Well, my mom being snatched out of our lives abruptly changed a lot of things, you know? Panic that she could be dead, and knowing that the only one who knew all the answers was God." Trevor's father, Rex ,had always had faith in God, and they'd gone to church as a family.

Trevor sighed. "The pastor one time said that hard times will either drive us far from God or towards God. I would rather be driven to God, since I can't control things, although I tend to forget that He's in control."

"Yeah, I've been feeling more driven towards God lately, and now that my grandma…" Her voice faded to a whisper and her lips trembled. Moisture formed in her eyes.

Oh boy! Trevor thought since he didn't think he was any good at comforting an emotional woman. He usually told his sister to suck it up whenever she cried. But with Keisha, her tears were caused by her hormonal changes. Very different from Sofia, who was hurting because she'd lost the most important person in her life.

Unsure of what to do, Trevor ran a hand over Sofia's back softly, stroking back and forth until her emotions settled.

They talked for almost an hour before the loud clunking of an engine interrupted them and clouds of dust billowed past the window. Enrique barged in, looking frazzled. "There you are!" he said, his chest heaving.

Trevor glanced at the watch on his wrist. It was five minutes past noon. Lunchtime was busy at the restaurant Enrique worked at during the day.

He rose and walked a few inches closer to Enrique. "What are you doing here when you're supposed to be helping your folks at the restaurant?"

Enrique adjusted the sunglasses that were perched on his forehead. His light skin glistened with sweat, and his white button-up shirt was damp. The guy was always overdressed except for their morning runs and when he wore his police uniform.

"I need you to help me arrest my grandma," he said, rubbing his eyes with his hand.

Integrity was one of the things Trevor liked about Enrique. No wonder they were a great team; they both loved justice.

Trevor opened his mouth, but then closed it since he wasn't sure how to respond just yet.

"Why?" he finally asked.

"She's been causing a ruckus at the Tavern." The Tavern was owned by a European couple who'd moved to Eron seven years ago.

Enrique threw his hands in the air. "I mean, she's been throwing glasses at the wall and yelling at the bartender whenever they tell her she's had enough to drink, and no one wants to be near her when she's drunk, trust me."

The problem with living in a small town was that Trevor knew almost everyone at a personal level, so when he made arrests, it was either his family or friends. And that was always the toughest part.

Trevor ran a hand over his face. He hated doing that. "When would you like me to do that?"

"Tonight. She's usually there by ten. I would rather not arrest her myself. Otherwise, I would never hear the end of it from the family."

Enrique sighed and his gaze shifted to Sofia as if he'd just noticed the third person in their midst.

"The pretty lady shows up again, yeah?" He blew Sofia a kiss.

Trevor punched him playfully in the stomach with his elbow and turned his gaze to Sofia, who wore a bemused smile as she stared at both of them.

"Arresting his grandma, huh? Did she make too many offensive needle points?" Sofia said.

He laughed. "You'd be surprised what the woman is capable of."

CHAPTER 7

Trevor sat on one of the red chairs by the creek behind his family's brick house. It was his favorite place to relax in the summertime, mostly because of the incredible view of the rolling green meadows vibrant with pink and purple daisies.

He'd always loved Eron's beautiful countryside, with its several creeks and a lake. The abundance of water and pasture had been an irresistible lure for early farmers and ranchers to settle there with their animals.

With his feet sprawled on the table, Trevor watched an elk in the distance grazing in a meadow of colorful wildflowers. He could see the foundation of the house he was having built on the same six-acre property as his childhood home. He hoped to get it fully built within three years.

Trevor loved Sundays for more than one reason; not only was it his day off from work, but it also gave him an opportunity to go to church with his family and worship with other believers..

His eyes lingered on the rugged mountains that were framed with a bright blue sky. That was another great thing about the town—Eron was surrounded by mountains and you could see them at every angle. Although some homes had a better view than others, Trevor was still grateful for the vantage point he had, and thankful for Eron in general. Being born and raised in Eron, perhaps he had nowhere else to compare it to.

After his mom went missing, Trevor knew that the one thing he wanted to do was become a detective, so he'd done everything in his power to receive the education and skills required for the job and was now one of the top detectives on the force.

His mother's body had never been found, and Trevor was determined to use his position to find out what had happened to her. He was more like doubting Thomas, whom he had just read about in the Bible—he had to find his mother's body before he could accept that she was truly gone, just like Thomas had to see

Jesus to believe in his resurrection. It was hard to mourn the loss of someone when you weren't quite sure if that's what you should be doing. Yet, at the same time, he held very little hope that his mother was still alive. Whatever had happened, he needed answers. Not only for his own satisfaction, but to get his mother the justice she deserved.

Thankful for the afternoon off, he read his Bible to reflect on the pastor's teaching earlier.

The sound of the gentle stream and the birds chirping were comforting as he flipped the pages of his Bible.

When he was done, he closed it and his mind started wandering to all sorts of things, mostly where it shouldn't go, and that was to the last person he should be thinking of—Sofia Wise. She was everything he shouldn't desire, but despite that, his mind kept bringing her up.

It had been almost a month since Sofia had come into his life. Trevor still couldn't understand what exactly he was doing with her, and he doubted the wisdom in seeing her. All he knew was that talking to her made him incredibly happy, happier than he had felt in a long time. Even more than his mom's comfort had made him.

Trevor had spent so much time talking to Sofia via chats and phone calls that he'd backed off from his mother's case. That was an achievement in itself. Besides the texts, Sofia had stopped by the station for a few surprise visits, and he'd run into her at the grocery store three days ago.

She'd been having more spiritual conversations with Trevor lately but was still hesitant to make it to church. Trevor always attended the second service with his family and hoped Sofia could join them one of these days. He would be willing to attend the early service on her account if that would get her to go.

Trevor had been contemplating asking her out on a date—problem was, he hadn't gone on any date in years and he didn't know if that would be a smart move. He hadn't even gathered the nerve to tell Keisha or his dad about Sofia. He shook his head, frustrated at his own cowardice.

"Thinking about your lady friend?" His father's voice caught him off guard. He jumped and turned.

Even with his mom gone, Trevor's dad still made sure they maintained their weekly Sunday dinners as a family like they used to do when their mom was still around. Since Sunday was the only day Trevor didn't have to work, and Keisha usually didn't have plans or homework, the family made a point of having lunch together on Sundays. They'd stuffed themselves with the chicken and baked macaroni and cheese that Keisha had made, and were now relaxing, with full stomachs.

Losing their mother had been hard on Trevor, but he imagined his father, Rex, had it equally tough. Jayla's disappearance had probably added five more years to his old man. Rex's once smooth black skin was pale, and his beard and hair were more gray than black. The tragedy had reminded them all how fragile life was, so it made sense that Trevor and Keisha made the time to hang out and talk to each other.

Trevor lowered his gaze to his intertwined fingers and shook his head, a tiny smile forming on his lips. "Nah, Dad," he responded simply.

Rex lowered himself onto the chair across from Trevor. "Your lips say no, but your eyes say something different." He studied Trevor for some seconds. "You know, if you want to talk about it, I'm a good listener," he offered.

Trevor shook his head in confusion. He wasn't even sure himself what was going on with Sofia—how would he make his father understand? It was common knowledge that Rex didn't feel malice toward the Wise family, certainly not the way Trevor felt. Rex wasn't mad at Sofia's family one bit, and if he was, then he had a very good way of hiding his feelings.

When Jayla had first gone missing, Rex had stated that he didn't think the Wise family was responsible for the disappearance of his wife. Trevor was miffed at the time that his father would exonerate them so easily. He still held that belief, but they kept it out of their conversations these days. Maybe that put his father in a better position to give some good advice, or maybe it didn't. He'd told his dad that he'd met a pleasant lady who was new in town. He hadn't given him further details.

Rex nodded in acknowledgment of Trevor's response. He stared out into the setting sun, allowing silence to envelop them for a while.

"I hear Sofia Wise is back in town," Rex said nonchalantly, but the meaning was clear.

Trevor knew that his dad had heard some rumors of him being seen with Sofia, but he hadn't been comfortable telling Rex about her.

His dad joined all his senior friends for game nights once a week at the Recreation Center, but Trevor knew they did more than just play games. Gossiping was the main event.

Trevor's muscles felt tense, and he fidgeted, trying to come up with a response.

"So I've heard," he replied dryly.

"I have to admit, son, you're very good at hiding your emotions, and if you weren't my son, I probably wouldn't have been able to read you as well as I do." He asked pointedly, "Is that all you got to say?"

Trevor shrugged. "What else am I supposed to say?"

Rex sank into one of the chairs and faced Trevor. "I guess I better stop beating around the bush instead of having what is promising to be an endless back and forth," Rex said, his face more serious. "Boy, you are a product of my blood, and you think I wouldn't know what's got you in a twist? I can read you like the back of my hand. The last time you got like this was when you were fifteen and wanted to ask Leah Granger to the school dance. Now, I'm aware that you have interacted with all the young females in Eron and you've been fine. Then pretty little Sofia Wise skips into town and you're suddenly interested in staring out into the sun? You don't fool me, boy, not one bit. Half the town knows you two are a couple, just thought I'd let you know." He took a deep breath. "Oh, and your pictures are already on Instagram," he added with a satisfied grin.

Trevor felt his resistance break as his father's words tore through his shield. Not that the guy even held an Instagram account, since he could barely navigate his cell phone.

Trevor let out a long sigh and he buried his face in his hands. He supposed he would have to spill his guts at this point—maybe his father would help him understand his feelings better. "She's in my head, Dad, but what if ..." His words faltered. A thought was nagging at him, but he wasn't quite able to put it into words. His father sat quietly, with a hand on his chin as if waiting for him to complete his words.

"....what if it's a setup?" he asked softly, his words barely audible

It was a suspicion that had been lingering in his mind from the moment his friendship with Sofia started. Everything in him screamed to shut her out, but his heart begged him not to listen. It whispered things like, *Asking her to church isn't going to ruin your investigation*, or i*t's okay to send text messages*. But he had to face the truth—since she'd come into his life, he'd slowed down on investigating his mother's disappearance. His mind was no longer consumed by it, but he knew he couldn't blame her for that. He could have easily been drawn to someone else, but that someone so happened to be a Wise. Could she be trusted? He wanted to believe so, but what if this was their plan all along?

Rex nodded in understanding. "The thing with relationships is that you should never go in with high expectations, but don't go in without a level of trust in the other person, either. If you really like this girl, give it a try. She's not her parents or her brother, she's her. Stop thinking everyone in the Wise family is coming for your head. Sofia never knew your mom and she's not a part of this thing you have with her family. Don't make her an enemy, and don't make yourself a victim of your own assumptions."

Trevor couldn't remember the last time he and his father had such a discussion, where his dad got the opportunity to give him advice on his personal life. It was certainly before his mother's disappearance. Come to think of it, he'd never had a romantic relationship since his teenage years. Regardless of where things were headed between him and Sofia, he was glad that his dad felt comfortable giving him personal advice. He allowed a smile to light up his features. "Thanks, Dad."

Rex returned his smile as he rose from his seat and patted Trevor's back. "You're welcome, Son."

As he said his prayers that night, Trevor yet again asked God what he should do about Sofia. Should he pursue her, or be cautious about letting her in? And just like the first time he prayed about her, he felt secure and safe, as if he was actually supposed to let her in. Trevor just wasn't sure if that was his own needs demanding attention, or God truly guiding him. He had to admit, with everything going on in his mind regarding his mother's disappearance, he had been having a hard time discerning the Spirit in his life. He'd been putting words and ideas in God's mouth, justifying his obsession lately, so that he'd forgotten what God's voice really sounded like. Come to think of it, had he ever known how God's voice sounded?

CHAPTER 8

Sofia blinked at the message that had popped up on her phone screen. Her face split open in a wide smile and her stomach boiled with new emotion.

It was a simple enough question—he was asking if she would like to go out to dinner with him soon. How cute that he had used the term 'dinner' rather than the more familiar one of 'date.' At least that's what she assumed this was.

It had been just over a month since she and Trevor had known each other, and she had been eagerly waiting for him to ask this question for a while now, but it still came as something of a surprise to her. Somewhere in her mind, she'd believed he would be restrained by the cold war between himself and her family members. She had imagined he would cease any communication with her one day, but having him ask her on a date was taking things to a new level which made her churn with excitement.

As soon as she got over the surprise, she typed her response:

Would love to.

She had barely hit "send" when her phone dinged with another message.

Saturday okay?

She grinned at her phone screen and replied:

Yes, Saturday is perfect.

I will pick you up no later than six p.m.

Where are we going?

It's a surprise.

Sofia stared at her phone with a goofy smile. She loved surprises. Even more, a surprise from the detective. She couldn't believe the sparks the detective ignited in her. She hadn't been so lucky in New York, perhaps because of her tight schedule, or maybe because most guys she encountered there reminded her of her family—career-driven, wealth driven and self-centered.

She liked Trevor, or maybe the fact that he wasn't her family's favorite gave her reason to like him even more.

"And what's got you so giddy?" Her mother's voice interrupted her blissful state.

Sofia dropped her phone and her eyes met her mother's smiling face as Marissa lowered herself onto a chair opposite her. Sofia's smile wiped off almost immediately.

"Nothing," she responded in a flat voice. She had yet to tell anyone in her family about her latest catch in the person of Trevor Freeman. She knew Brent suspected it, but so far, he had not yet uttered a word to anyone else, and she wanted to keep it that way. She would tell them about Trevor when she felt the time was right. She didn't need any of her selfish family members ruining everything before she got to experience it.

Her mother cocked her brow. "Really? For a second there, I could have sworn you were reading something pretty interesting on that phone of yours. Might it be private discussions with a man?" she asked with a mischievous smile.

Sofia shook her head. "Mother, not everything has to be about a man."

Marissa pursed her lips at those words, and Sofia could see the lecture coming even before she said a word. Marissa was very predictable, and Sofia knew her very well.

Marissa forced a smile. "Darling, you're twenty-five years old. At your age, I was pregnant with your brother."

Sofia rolled her eyes, "Wasn't that like, thirty years ago?"

Marissa looked a bit offended that her daughter had responded in that manner, but Sofia couldn't help herself. She was sick of the comparisons; she definitely wasn't her mother, and didn't want to be.

Marissa needed to get with the program and stop trying to fulfill whatever unfulfilled fantasies she harbored through Sofia's life. It was disheartening that after all this time, the people she called family still didn't understand her and wouldn't give her the space she merited.

Rather than lash out at her, Sofia chose to study her phone instead.

"Sofia, darling," Marissa said. "You're a brilliant young woman with a successful career, one that any man in his right senses would want to be associated with. For the life of me, I can't understand why you're still single. You should be attracting the attention of all the prestigious eligible bachelors."

Sofia stared at her mother blankly.

"Honey, what's wrong?" Marissa asked, her face contorting in what could only be described as confusion.

"Let me stop you right there." Sofia closed her eyes as memories washed over her, causing her stomach to knot up. "Remember Warren, eleven years ago?"

Marissa's face went pale and she nodded, her eyes drifting to some distant place.

"I still carry that memory around. I'm not upset with him so much as I am with my own family. For not standing up for me when you should've." Sofia shuddered as she relived the horrific scene in her mind. She'd been only fourteen when it happened.

Almost every weekend, there had been a party at the Wise house. This particular evening, Sofia had made her escape to her bedroom. As she lay on the bed reading, the door was flung open. She whirled around to see a guy in his twenties stagger into her room. Warren was the son of one of her family's business associates, but he'd never been friendly toward Sofia.

Terrified, she jumped off the bed. "You're not supposed to be in here," she said frantically, in a shaky voice.

Warren leered at her. His breath reeked of alcohol. "Yeah, I know."

He grabbed her hand and pulled her closer. Panicked, Sofia struggled to break away, but the slim teenager was no match for a full-grown man. He cupped her head with a rough hand and leaned in to kiss her.

Something snapped in Sofia then, and she screamed, at the same time jerking her knee up to strike him in the crotch. She sighed with relief when Warren released her. He left the room, groaning and cursing.

No one came in response to her scream—the music from the bottom floor was loud, but surely someone had heard her. What if Warren came back?

She forced her shaking legs to carry her to the door. She shut it again firmly, locking it this time. Then she flung herself onto her bed and sobbed while the party went on downstairs. Nobody even knew anything had happened to her, and she lay in her room wide awake for the rest of the night.

The first thing she did the next day was to tell her mother what had happened. Her mother's indifferent response still bothered Sofia even now.

"Warren would never take it too far. His dad is a close friend of your father's," Marissa had said, making excuses and downplaying the significance of the situation. That was when Sofia had come to the conclusion that her house wasn't safe.

She'd moved in with her grandma for the rest of that school year until she'd asked to leave for New York.

"Darling, I didn't think it was that bad at the time until I told your brother about it after you left for New York. For the first time, Brent lost it. Two days later, he came home with a black eye." Marissa shook her head. "He told me he'd showed up at Warren's place of work and punched him—turned out Warren hit him harder, and Brent was escorted out by the police. Thankfully, the guy didn't sue him."

Sofia's jaw dropped open and her hand went to her heart. She was so touched that at least her brother had stepped up on her behalf, something she'd never have expected from Brent. Not only was he a terrible fighter, but he'd always seemed to care only for himself.

She let that sink in for a second. "Did Brent really do that?"

"Yes, and once your father got involved, that was the end of his friendship with Warren's dad."

Sofia took a deep breath and sank further into the couch, her face buried in her hands..

Marissa swung her hands dismissively.

"So Warren was a jerk, but that doesn't mean that every rich guy is like him." She crossed one leg over the other, oblivious to Sofia's reaction. Marissa edged closer to her seat and smiled at her.

Sofia's stomach roiled. Whatever her mother was getting ready to say, she knew she wouldn't like it.

She thought of making a hasty exit, but before her decision was made, Marissa's mouth opened.

"I was thinking ..." She tapped her finger on her chin. "We have a meeting coming up at the country club, and I have this friend of mine, Charlene, her son just returned from Europe. He's an engineer, twenty-seven years old. Maybe we can connect you two and you can both take it from there."

Of course. There it was again, the pitch, the reason for her mother disturbing her day. This was the sole ambition of Marissa Wise, to marry her daughter off to the first, rich, snobby kid to hop off a plane. Sofia should have known her mother wasn't interested in them talking as girls, she was interested in convincing Sofia to date a guy who fit her own description of perfect.

She'd heard enough, and, had honestly, seen enough of her mother's chemically enhanced face to last her another three days. Here she was, on a high after Trevor asked her out, and this woman had just come in here to ruin that high with her ridiculous antics.

She got to her feet and stared at her mother, debating the wisdom of telling her the truth. She could just bottle up her issues with Marissa's attitude and go into her room as she used to as a teenager; that would save them a lot of stress and at least maintain their cordial relationship. Or, she could stop being a coward and tell her mother just where her opinion was irrelevant. She settled on the latter.

Taking a long, deep breath, she let her words fly out. "I'm not a child, Mother. I don't need you to set up any dates for me, and my love life is just fine. I don't remember making any complaints to you about it, but when I do have one, you'll be the first to hear it. Now, may I please leave?"

Her mother's jaw dropped open as if so mortified at her words that all she could do was stare at her with her mouth slightly agape.

Without waiting for her mother to recover from the sting of her words, Sofia marched out of the living room. She had a date with Trevor Freeman in three days and needed some time planning her outfit. She was by all means going, and she wasn't about to let her mother's meddling ways ruin her excitement.

***

The day had finally come for their planned date, and Trevor was as nervous as he'd been on the day of his first school dance, which he had planned to go to with Leah, the girl he'd had a crush on. The only difference between Leah and Sofia was that Trevor was a little more confident in himself at the moment that he'd been back then, and things would probably turn out for the best tonight, unlike that awful night.

He hadn't gone with Leah to the dance as planned. In fact, he hadn't gone at all. He'd reached the front of the school and waited for her, only to see her coming with some other guy, Freddie Marcus. Freddie was the most popular kid in school back then, and rumors had been rife about whether or not Freddie would make it to the dance after he'd sprained his ankle while playing basketball. The story was that he wouldn't come, and Trevor surmised that Leah had only agreed to go with him based on that rumor. However, Freddie had recovered just in time for the dance, and Trevor was the inevitable loser in it all. It had been quite a heartbreaking experience for him, and he had skipped school for an entire week after it.

Today though, there was no Freddie Marcus, and Sofia wasn't Leah ... well, he hoped not. While there was no Freddie, there was an entire family that could ruin his day as well, and he would only have his father to run back to this time, and not the soothing words of his mother.

Sofia had suggested they meet at the venue instead, so as not to ruin their night with him coming to her house to pick her up, seeing as how that would have raised more than a few brows and maybe even caused an altercation. While Trevor was a man who loved to keep to the rules of engagement for the average gentleman, he couldn't agree more that theirs was a peculiar case, and he would have to forfeit the tradition of picking her up from her parent's home. That's why he'd ordered an Uber driver to go after Sofia in his place.

He looked down at his wristwatch as he stood by the entrance to wait for her. If he couldn't pick her up from her home, they could at least walk in together. He had made a reservation at a very classy restaurant, one that many would probably opine was way beyond whatever his family could afford, but he had done it for a reason. He wanted to take Sofia to a place that might be more her style.

At least it was within his means. Besides saving money for his house to be built, he'd saved up a separate fund just for special occasions, and if he could consider anything special, this was it. He was grateful for the savings, because, knowing Sofia's upbringing, it wouldn't do to take her anywhere beneath her status, and this place was just right.

Their dinner reservations were made for seven pm, and it was just a few minutes before that time. He knew it was a ridiculous fear, but Trevor found himself hoping and praying that she would show up. When they'd spoken over the phone, Sofia had seemed excited about it. Surely, she wouldn't stand him up.

Before he took another look at his wristwatch, a cab stopped in front of the restaurant and Sofia stepped out. A long sigh of relief escaped his lungs; he hadn't realized he'd been holding his breath. She smiled at him and waved, and Trevor walked over to pay the middle-aged man.

Sofia dug a wallet from her purse "Trevor, it's fine, I'll pay."

He shook his head, pulling a fifty dollar bill out of his wallet. "I invited you, remember?" Trevor said and leaned down to hand money to the cab driver. "Keep the change."

The guy smiled and nodded his appreciation. Trevor stood to his full height and the car drove off.

Sofia smiled at him. "Thank you." Seeing her genuine smile took away all the knots in his stomach, and the anxiety he was dealing with.

He returned her smile. "You're welcome." He linked his hand with hers. "Shall we?"

Sofia winked and locked arms with him. "Of course."

As they made their way into the restaurant together, Trevor braced himself against the stares directed their way. He was painfully aware of the suspicious looks several of the diners cast over him as he walked by with Sofia. Not many African-Americans frequented this place, so Trevor could understand why he might stand out, but the attention made him feel awkward, uncomfortable. He already felt like he was out of his league dating Sofia—he didn't need this reminder of their differences. He began to wonder if this had been such a good idea. Maybe he was kidding himself.

He shook off his doubts. He was with Sofia, and that was all that mattered at the moment. "By the way, you look stunning in that dress." As he said it, he knew that truer words had never been spoken. She had on a green sequined dress that reached her calf and hugged her petite but curvy frame, on her feet were a pair of silver, five-inch heeled sandals with ankle straps, and her hair was swept up in an elegant up-do. She looked like she belonged in the pages of a magazine. He almost felt underdressed next to her.

He didn't own a suit and had decided to settle for a pair of khaki pants, with a button-up shirt and a black sport coat.

"You look handsome yourself," she said with a warm smile.

Now seated with menus on the table, Trevor took a moment to look at the interior of the restaurant. It looked like one of those places he'd seen in movies. There was unique artwork on the wall, accented by soft lighting, and the white tablecloths were starched and spotless. And the people inside the restaurant were all dressed up as if they were going to an opera of some kind.

He flipped open his menu, studying it.

Goodness, who pays this much for a salad?

Sofia was studying her menu in silence as if this was nothing out of the ordinary for her. Trevor had to do some mental math and realized the salad cost as much as a pair of tennis shoes for him.

"What are you having?" she asked.

Trevor hadn't even looked over the entire menu. Not only were the food choices listed unfamiliar, but the prices didn't make his decision any easier.

But then he was here for Sofia. He hoped they wouldn't be eating dinner here often because this kind of lifestyle was way out of his reach. He made a decent check, but not enough extra to splurge on this kind of luxury.

"What do you recommend?" he said, trying to remind himself that he was in this room with the most gorgeous girl on the planet.

Once he decided to enjoy Sofia's company, his shoulders relaxed.

"Beef Pot-au-Feu, they can't ever go wrong with that," Sofia said.

Why they had to give complex names to a stew of some kind, Trevor would never understand. At this point, he was past the thought of focusing on the cost.

"All right then, beef it is."

The waiter returned with hors-d'oeuvres and took their order.

They chatted easily while they waited to be served. Sofia laughed a lot, especially when he told her about the time his sister had played a prank on him three years ago since he was afraid of snakes. She'd placed a toy snake under his pillow. "It looked so real, and I came out of my bed screaming like a ten-year-old."

He couldn't help but notice how comfortable Sofia felt with him. He took in her appearance. Her make-up was mostly light, her lips glossy. She'd added something smoky to her eyelids, and it brought out her hazel irises nicely. She was the most beautiful woman he'd ever seen. He hoped the rest of their evening would be just as beautiful.

CHAPTER 9

Sofia laughed at a joke Trevor had made. It was one of many laughs he had coaxed from her over the last thirty minutes of being in his company. It had been a while since she'd laughed this hard. For months, she'd been overwhelmed with work; that's why she'd agreed to make the trip to Africa. And then the loss of her grandmother—well, laughing didn't seem possible some days. Grateful for Trevor's witty commentary and ridiculous jokes, she finally felt completely at ease. Sofia felt as if she could truly breathe, without the weight of her family and grief for her grandma weighing on her.

Sofia couldn't completely ignore the roadblock that stood in the middle of their potential relationship, though. She still found it hard to reconcile Trevor's fun personality to that hard-faced man who had walked into their house six weeks ago and caused a stir. To discover that such a comedian was hiding behind all of that masculinity was an eye-opener. Perhaps they could work through what stood in their way. Sofia knew her family was harsh, crazy, and did a lot of questionable things—but they would never physically harm anyone. And though she never would expect anyone of her choosing to accept her family, she never expected someone would believe her parents to be responsible for anyone's disappearance.

"I swear, I had never felt dumber in my life," he stated.

She giggled and rolled her eyes, letting him know she didn't believe he was dumb at all.

He had just relayed to her a story about a bust gone wrong. Based on a tip from some anonymous guy about a stash of drugs that were being moved out of New Mexico, Trevor and his team had gone after the truck in which the drugs were purportedly being transported, only to finally capture it and find it filled with potatoes.

"I bet you screen every tip you get these days with an extra eye."

"Of course I do. There is no way I'll be fooled like that again."

She smiled as she reached for her glass of water and took a sip. They had completely ignored the hors-d'oeuvres before them, since they were so lost in each other's company.

Sofia had to admit she had been a bit surprised when she found out this was where they were having their date. The restaurant was newly opened and their menu prices were somewhat high for such a small town. And though she appreciated this kind of effort, she hoped it wasn't putting too much of a hole in his pocket. Sofia wasn't blind to the lifestyle of others. Many of her college friends had been scholarship students, struggling to make rent and buy food, living off of Top Ramen for most of the semesters.

When she'd asked about his choice of restaurant, Trevor had told her he brought her here to support a French couple that had moved to Eron a year ago. She was glad he hadn't done it just to impress her, although she couldn't help but admire the place.

The restaurant had risen quickly to become a favorite for the crème de la crème of Colorado. Everything was top quality and worth every penny.

In the half an hour they'd been there, they had spoken about everything from their high school experiences to their experiences at work. When Trevor had told her about his family, he spoke about his little sister with so much joy. Sofia could tell he adored her just by the way his face lit up whenever he mentioned her name. Although her mother often pushed her in the direction of wealthy pigs that she called suitable men, Sofia could recall one piece of advice her mother told her at a young age. Her mother had said, "You can always tell how a man will treat his wife by the way he cares for his sister." Though she always thought it silly, because her brother had teased her more than protected her growing up. But after what her mom had shared with her three days ago, maybe her brother did protect her in his own way.

While Trevor discussed his concerns and hopes for his little sister, Sofia, on the other hand, had barely spoken of her family. It wasn't just because she didn't adore them the way Trevor seemed to adore his, but also because every one of them struck the wrong chord in him, and if she were to bring them up, it would probably stir up too many other things. Her family was the elephant in the room, and she knew that at some point they would have to address the fact that she was part of the family he despised so much. At some point, they would have to work through this—but could they? Sofia pushed the question away, because tonight she wanted to enjoy Trevor's presence, to enjoy the attention this man gave her, his smile, and that look of longing in his eyes.

Sofia wasn't oblivious, though. She had taken the opportunity to do a Google search on Jayla Freeman the day before, and the story of her disappearance had come up. She already knew bits and pieces from what her parents had told her and what she had seen on the news in the past. Trevor's mother was believed to be dead and the prime suspects were Sofia's parents. Investigations had been going on for years, but neither Jayla nor her body had ever been found. A lawsuit was pending against Sofia's parents, with the claim that they were hiding evidence.

The internet search had given Sofia only surface information though; only what the tabloids knew of the case, not what the actual actors in it knew. Trevor's mother had begun working as a housekeeper in the Wise home about the time Sofia had moved to New York to live with her aunt.

Jayla's son was still pursuing justice, which had been obvious from Trevor's appearance at her parents' house. Sofia couldn't fault him for that, even if it was her own family he suspected. After all, she would have done the same if a member of her family had gone missing like that.

As they settled into a smooth conversation, Sofia figured she would venture a little further to inquire about his mother's disappearance. She knew it was a dangerous topic, but she couldn't seem to help herself. No matter how hard she tried to focus on the date itself, her mind kept going back to that roadblock.

They would have to talk about her family at some point, and she needed to understand his perspective.

"So, what's your deal with my family? I know they can be difficult to deal with, but you seem to have a lot of issues with them."

Trevor's face froze for a moment. He sighed and stared down at the table, as if trying to decide what to say. Maybe she shouldn't have asked. After all, he was a detective on the case, and there might be legal reasons they shouldn't be talking about it.

"To be honest, I just want my mother back, and the only minor evidence I have points to your family." He opened his mouth as if to say something else, seemed to think about it before he closed it.

She allowed his words to sink in and chose her next ones with care. "I know she went missing after work, but do you think, maybe, my parents really had nothing to do with that? They are a lot of things, but murderers?" She felt sick at the idea and wondered how

Trevor could even entertain such a thought. Yet he was still here having dinner with her. She wondered why.

"If they had nothing to do with her disappearance, I'm sure we'll find out soon," he responded evenly.

Sofia managed a smile as she decided to drop the topic. There was no use trying to convince the man that he was wrong, and any such attempts would lead to an otherwise great outing being abruptly cut short, and she simply couldn't have that. "Sure," she replied.

She might not be on the best of terms with her family, and sure, they behaved a bit sketchy when it came to questions about the pending investigation, but somehow she knew her family wasn't responsible for his mother's disappearance. Her family may behave like a bunch of spoiled rich jerks, but they weren't killers. Far from it. However, she was also aware that it was hard to change a man's mind once he had it made up, and this was one of those times. Only strong evidence would convince Trevor that he had the wrong people, and she knew that evidence would surface with time. Sofia had faith in that—she only hoped that his faith in her would last that long. She could see the questioning look in his eyes.

"So, you're part Swedish?" he asked, changing the subject.

"Yeah, my grandparents moved here from Sweden, according to my grandma's knowledge. They had my parents in the US and they'd settled in Eron."

"Swedish, huh?" he asked absentmindedly and shook his head as if to clear it before he spoke again. "So, tell me more about your life in New York."

No doubt, he was only trying to divert the discussion from the almost sour turn it had taken, and Sofia appreciated that attempt. It meant he saw beyond her family name and was still very much interested in her as a person. "Well, you're in luck. I think I will have a couple of good stories," she replied.

"By all means, please share." A male voice from behind her suddenly interrupted their discussion.

Sofia felt herself grow cold. She knew that voice even in her sleep. If she was somehow mistaken about that, the look on Trevor's face confirmed her fears. Brent had to be standing directly behind her; she could even smell his cologne. What in the name of all things sane is he doing here?

Brent finally emerged from behind her to stand between them, but his hard eyes were on her, and she could tell he felt she'd betrayed him somehow. Knowing she'd disappointed her brother was something she was used to, but there was this strange new feeling that seized her....was it guilt?.

"Great seeing you here, Sis. What might you be doing here? Aside from fraternizing with the enemy, of course," he said in a voice laden with false sweetness.

On any other day, Sofia would probably have taken up her brother's challenge and sent some witty words back to him. But the knowledge of her brother standing up for her years ago, something he hadn't bothered to share with her, was still fresh in her mind. She was going to lay low with him for as long as her patience could hold. "What are you doing here?" she asked, her voice far lower than his.

"I came to have dinner with my fiancée. You know ..." His stern gaze turned to Trevor. "The one who's not accusing our entire family of murder?"

"Brent, there's no need to cause a scene," Trevor addressed Sofia's brother calmly.

"You would do well to be quiet while I'm addressing my sister, detective," he spoke the word so snidely even Sofia felt the sting. But if she thought Brent was done with them, she had another thing coming. He turned his attention to her once again. "You know, when you said you didn't have a love life, I thought it was a cause for concern, but I never thought you were so desperate you would reduce yourself to dating the housekeeper's son."

CHAPTER 10

Trevor could only wonder that their night had not come to an abrupt end following all of the drama that had happened in a matter of minutes.

Brent's appearance had almost put a dent on the evening for him. He had been so close to losing his cool and doing something stupid, but he was thankful for Sofia's presence. It had been the calming agent he needed. He had to admit, she had surprised him a lot today—not only had she stood by him despite her brother's attacks, she had also ignored those attacks enough to remain with him after Brent had left. He had expected her to make up some weak excuse and runoff, but she pulled through the night, acting like they hadn't had a heated confrontation with her brother in the restaurant.

Sofia held onto his arm as they gazed into the stars, seated on the blanket from the back of his beat-up red Toyota truck. Despite the truck's rugged look, Sofia had ridden in it without giving it a second glance. She'd asked him what he did for fun, and while he didn't have a long list of that, stargazing was something he had always loved. He figured she had earned a ticket to indulge in his guilty pleasures.

Trevor thought of the conversation they'd shared the first time Sofia had visited him at work. She'd seemed to want to share more about her reason for leaving, but had switched the conversation out of the blue. Probably nothing had happened, but he had a gut instinct and he'd been curious to know the whole story since. Was tonight the best time for such details? He had planned to save personal questions for another time.

"Did something happen to you… and caused you to leave Eron?"

The words came out of his mouth before he let his mind process what he was going to say. Sofia jumped and moved her hand to her chest. Trevor opened his mouth to tell her to forget his question, but Sofia spoke first.

"Why do you think anything happened?" she asked. It was hard to make out her facial expression with only the natural light from the stars above.

"Just a feeling," he said dismissively, as if not too interested, and allowed the silence to linger in case she was considering sharing anything.

She took a deep breath. "Well, uh- remember when I told you I hated the parties my family hosted every weekend?"

Trevor braced himself for what was coming, even though he didn't think he would like to hear it. "Yeah, I remember."

Sofia told him about Warren, leaving nothing out of the story. Trevor listened as he impatiently stroked her back, encouraging her to keep talking. He felt her shiver and he ripped off his blazer, wrapping it around her.

Proud of her bravery in fighting off a drunk at age fourteen, he held her shoulders to face her even though he could see no more than a silhouette with the light of a half moon. He turned and pressed a kiss to her forehead, "What happened to this Warren guy?" he said through gritted teeth, hoping that jerk was behind bars where he belonged. Otherwise, he would love a one on one session with that scumbag so he could teach him a thing or two about respecting women.

Sofia sighed. "It was a long time ago, and there was no evidence…" she trailed off, putting her face in her hands.

"At least my brother tried, although he's not as good a fighter, as much as he loves stirring up fights with his tongue."

Trevor took a deep breath, thankful that Brent had at least wanted some retribution for his sister's attacker. Unlike Marissa's reaction. That part didn't surprise Trevor for a second—the woman was a gold digger, but again that was Trevor's point of view, although he didn't think Sofia would disagree.

"I have more respect for your brother now." At least for Sofia's sake, Trevor might start seeing Brent in a different light. In the meantime, this Warren guy was going on his list of people to investigate. A background search wouldn't hurt.

Sofia's head was leaning against his chest and he had his hand wrapped around her shoulder. He felt the urge to protect her and fight her physical battles for her, even against her family if they acted like Marissa.

She snuggled against him and Trevor was only too willing to welcome her. It was the first time he'd ever held a woman like this. She was silent for a long time, watching the stars with deep wonder. Thankfully, the sky was filled with them tonight.

He'd just downloaded a stargazing app, and hoped to utilize his current knowledge.

"Do you see that?" he pointed to a constellation.

"I see a very bright star," she said, her warm breath sending goosebumps to the rest of his body.

"Yeah, that's Orion, one of the brightest and best-known constellations in the night sky," Trevor told her the origin of Orion, named after the hunter in Greek mythology.

They sighted two other constellations as Trevor answered Sofia's questions about stars in general. "Wow!" she whispered. "What is it about these stars that grasps your attention?" she asked after staring upward for a while.

Trevor shrugged. "I guess it's their unity. I like how each star is allowed to shine in its own way. There's an individuality about them, you don't have much of that among humans. Some stifle the shine of others, some block it completely, but humans generally do not like someone else taking up their shine. It brings out the worst in them."

"That's new. I don't think I've ever heard that perspective from stargazers."

"Well, you know what they say—every day you live, is another day to learn."

"Nah, I don't think I've heard that one."

Trevor chuckled softly and said, "Now you have."

They returned to a comfortable silence once again as they stared at the stars. It was far better than the tense silence back at the restaurant, and both of them were grateful for the shift in energy between them. Sofia couldn't help but think, So long as my family isn't involved, everything is fine. And though she understood why it pained her, because, after all— they were her family.

He felt her lean closer to him. "Trevor," she called.

"Hmm?"

"How have you been coping since your mother's disappearance?" she asked gently.

It was quite a sensitive question, but Trevor didn't have any issues with giving her a response. Since she'd shared an uncomfortable part of her past, she'd earned the right to ask all the questions she needed. "It's been quite the experience. I don't know if you've noticed, but I don't have a lot of friends, and I'm not as good with sharing my feelings with someone else as most people are. Recently, whenever I've felt really down, I've slowly learned to talk to God. I feel when I talk to him, He pulls me back in, gives me perspective, and helps me keep going."

She was quiet for a moment. "I would like to go to church service with you next Sunday. I can't go tomorrow because my family is getting together with some extended family members," she said. Her comment came out of the blue and Trevor couldn't hide his surprise.

"I didn't really like church very much as a kid, but I remember enjoying it whenever I went with my grandma."

"Church can be comforting," Trevor said. "I take it your dislike of church might have been influenced by your family's perspective about church?"

Sofia chuckled. "You know them so well."

Trevor smiled. "I've been keeping a keen eye on them for the last six years," he replied. "I don't want them to ruin your perspective of what it means to be in God's house. You are received with open arms." Although Trevor knew there would be curious stares on her first visit, the people at his church were genuinely kind and loving.

He'd attended this church for years and considered it his spiritual home, and the members were his family, but this was uncharted territory. Trevor had never invited a woman before, so him bringing any girl would tell the members that he wanted something special with her, to share his life with her. While Trevor couldn't deny he still had doubts about the inevitable barriers ahead if he pursued a relationship with Sofia, spending the entire evening with her had shown him a part of her that he was really interested in. Sofia wasn't like the rest of her family members, like his father had said. She was different—warm, kind, and happy. She was that breath of fresh air he hadn't known he needed until now.

As if reading his mind, she asked, "If we drive together to your church, would people think that we were getting married soon?" she teased.

Trevor laughed at her humor. It probably would seem that way to many of the members of the church; he could imagine some older members would ask such a question. Trevor tested the waters with the next question. "Would that be so bad?"

He felt her go still at those words. He didn't think much of it—it was only a tease, though he was curious as to her answer. Her sudden silence surprised him, though. Had he said something wrong? He hoped he hadn't jeopardized his chances with her just because of some silly words. Trevor squeezed her hand and she raised her head up to look at him—their eyes might have locked but it was hard to see each other in the dark.

Sofia seemed surprised by his words, but he hoped it was more of a positive surprise than a negative one, because before he could take back his words, Sofia turned and reached her hand up to cup his cheek. Her touch was filled with warmth that Trevor couldn't help but lean into. She tilted her head a bit higher until their lips touched. It was such a soft feeling, but it was all it took to send a charge of current zipping through Trevor's body. He bent and slid his hand around to the nape of her neck, pulling her in closer to deepen the kiss, welcoming the softness of her lips. She shuddered against him and he groaned, surprised by how much the kiss affected him.

He slowly pulled back, not wanting to be tempted any further. She did the same and leaned away from him.

He didn't need to look at her eyes to know they were still closed. Her breath was a bit uneven, considering they had been locking lips for over a minute.

"That was...." she sighed. She didn't need to say the words for Trevor to understand just what she meant, because he felt it through the loud pounding of his heart, and if it were daytime, he knew she would see it written all over his face, too. They were both filled with a passion so deep, if they didn't stop now, they wouldn't stop at all.

She lay her head back onto his chest and snuggled closer.

"Sofia," he spoke after a while.

"Hmm?"

"Thanks for tonight. It was amazing," he said, his words dripping with sincerity. Come to think of it, he'd never really kissed a girl before. After his dilemma with Leah, he'd treaded lightly with the next girl in high school. Being on the basketball team had made him popular with the girls, but he'd refrained from romance, since he didn't want love based on his popularity on the school team.

He'd never had the pleasure of having a night like this. It was quite the revealing night—he'd had no idea what effects would come from someone you were attracted to until now.

Trevor had built a cold wall around himself after his mother's disappearance, and the last person he'd expected to tear it down was a Wise … yet he couldn't be happier that he had shelved his doubts and asked her on a date. He could have missed out on an amazing woman.

***

Brent had yet to say a word to their parents about his discovery. Sofia knew that because if he had said something, they would have summoned her for proper questioning at some point. However, it was a whole week later and there wasn't so much as a word being mentioned about Trevor. The detective who seemed bent on discovering a secret that Sofia knew could not exist.

Everything was perfect with Trevor, except for the fact that he thought her family to be murderers. She sighed, thinking that perhaps no relationship is perfect, and perhaps that was the one epic flaw in this one.

It bothered Sofia that her brother hadn't said anything yet. She couldn't tell what Brent was playing at—if there was some hidden agenda and purpose, he was definitely keeping that information to himself. Maybe he planned to blackmail them. Whatever his reason was, he hadn't brought his finding to their parents. Strangely enough, it didn't deter Sofia's interest.

Her conversations with Trevor had become more meaningful and deep. He had even told her more about his mother's case, and she was starting to see that his doggedness was only to be expected from a child who wanted justice done for his mom. Besides, she figured there were a lot of details he was advised not to talk about. He wasn't simply being a bitter man looking to drag someone else down.

The next Sunday, Sofia got ready for church. Trevor had told her it was on the side of town her parents would turn their noses up at.

Her phone chimed just as she slid on some strappy, medium-heeled shoes. She glanced at the screen and saw Trevor's name. He'd sent a text to let her know that he had arrived and was waiting by the driveway. It was his way of avoiding a heated argument with any of her family members before church.

She took one last look at her bed and stared at the mound of clothes she'd yanked out of the closet in an attempt to find just the right outfit for church. Trevor had told her it didn't matter what she wore as long as she was coming to God's house, as long as it was decent, of course. She'd finally settled for a floral round skirt with a sea green top that she'd tucked in.

Thankful that her family was still asleep after their usual Saturday late night party, Sofia stepped out of the quiet house. On her way out, she waved to the older man, who was re-arranging things in the kitchen. "See you later, Louis."

"Have fun, Ms. Wise," was all Louis said. Sofia was thankful that he minded his own business, unlike her family that didn't know when to let her be.

Trevor was leaning against his truck, arms crossed, dressed in a short sleeve button-down shirt tucked into his jeans. He was staring at the mountains in the distance until the sound of her shoes clicking on the cobblestone drew his attention to her. He turned and smiled instantly at the sight of her. His smile melted her heart, and she smiled in return as he walked towards her.

"Hey," he greeted, planting a soft kiss on her forehead and another on her lips. She closed her eyes, and found herself encircling his neck with her hands, offering her mouth for more, and Trevor obliged.

"Sofia," Trevor said, his lips still resting against hers.

"Hmm?"

"Church." He placed another soft kiss on her lips.

"Oh. Yes. Church." She let her arms drop from his shoulders.

He took in her appearance, staring at her head to toe.

"I hope this outfit is perfect for church?" She managed to talk in a strained voice.

"Are you kidding me?" Trevor smiled, his brow cocked. "You're more than perfect. You look beautiful."

He took her hand and guided her the next few steps to the truck, opening the passenger door for her to get in.

Gospel music played softly on the radio as he drove. Sofia spent part of the time looking at the passing scenery and people. These were the people her parents would refer to as disreputable. They would cringe if they knew she had come here, especially after she'd declined going to their own church.

The drive to the church wasn't long. In a matter of minutes, they were parked in front of a modest, white building. Just by looking at the structure,

Sofia could tell the church had a lot of history behind it.

"We're here," Trevor announced with a smile.

She returned his smile, even though she was a bit nervous about going in. She hadn't been in a religious house in years, so it was bound to be awkward going into this one, especially as their mode of worship was sure to be different from what she was used to. At her family's church, everything felt watered down and quiet. She suspected this wasn't going to be a quiet worship experience.

Trevor reached out for her hand and squeezed it lightly. "It will be fine."

Those words were enough to give her the courage to step out of the truck when Trevor opened the door for her. As they walked to the church entrance together, she could hear singing from inside.

"Are you ready?" Trevor asked as he placed his hand on the door.

She tightened her grip on his hand and nodded. Sofia experienced a variety of emotions as she waited for Trevor to open the door. She was almost afraid to step into such a holy place, having not been all that religious growing up. She now felt like a wolf in sheep's clothing walking into a temple, but she knew that was a ridiculous thought. Trevor gave her another smile of encouragement as he opened the door, and she was overwhelmed by the beautiful sound of sonorous voices that wiped all the jitters from her tummy. This promised to be an enjoyable experience.

CHAPTER 11

The singing continued for several more heartfelt worship songs. Sofia closed her eyes and let the praises wash away any lingering doubts about being here. Soon the worship team was replaced by a gray-haired, black pastor.

The pastor gave an animated sermon about the difference between happiness and joy, describing how happiness was acquired temporarily when something happened to please us, but joy was given to us within, and could never be taken away from us, no matter our circumstances. Only God could give joy.

This was a much needed message for Sofia. Growing up in a wealthy family hadn't always been as stress-free as most would think. Sofia had had to compromise lots of times for the good of the family. Having been on her own these past ten years had helped her get another perspective on life.

She'd made a name for herself, creating her own successful business outside of those that were part of the Wise Empire. Yet she still felt her life was empty and missing something. That was another reason she'd returned home a changed person, and she hoped her family would be able to understand how her thinking worked now and accept it as well.

When she'd gone with a group of Christians who were teaching English to students in Burundi, Sofia had felt closer to God than she had in ages. Sofia's former college roommate Mandy had reached out to her and invited her to join the trip, long after Sofia had graduated from college. Sofia was grateful for Mandy's persistence in keeping in touch—she wasn't the average roommate.

Helping the needy—seeing the kid's faces filled with love and joy despite the fact they had no shoes and some wore ripped clothes—had given Sofia more happiness than anything else she'd experienced. The children had so little, yet they still had the most genuine smiles Sofia had ever witnessed.

Sofia could still see their faces when she closed her eyes at night. Working with the underprivileged had really touched her heart, and she'd started realizing money didn't buy happiness. She'd asked Trevor a few spiritual questions in the last few weeks, and between the small seeds that had been planted from the trip she'd taken and the random Christian people that had been in her life, Sofia had no doubt God was telling her something.

The service came to an end much earlier than Sofia would have liked. She'd been soaking in the message of today's sermon as it had reached to her core, pulling at her heartstrings. She'd enjoyed it immensely, which was saying a lot considering she usually found church services to be a bore-fest. This preacher, however, was lively and enthusiastic. He had an undeniable excitement about God and was fun to listen to.

All in all, today's service stirred something deep in Sofia's heart.

At the close of the service, the pastor invited people to come down the aisle for prayer, and for those who wanted everlasting joy through the transforming power of Christ to come and pray with one of the four other pastors at the altar.

Sofia's insides churned, and she felt a stirring to go for prayer, but when she opened her eyes and turned her head to see the house full of strangers, she figured it would have to be another time.

After offering baskets had been passed and the congregation dismissed, Sofia gathered her belongings. She'd asked Trevor if they could exit before the end of the service, since she'd wanted to avoid any interactions with the church people. Church was definitely not her usual hangout, yet she'd enjoyed it nonetheless. That's why she'd not been paying attention when the service ended.

As they exited the pew and walked down the aisle, Trevor was ambushed by an abrupt greeting from the people who'd sat behind them. Before Sofia could pick up her purse, a greeting from behind her caused her to turn to find a cheerful old woman waiting for her response.

Snapping out of it, Sofia formed a quick smile for the woman. "Oh, hi."

"Theda. I know you're Sofia Wise," the woman said.

Her mouth opened in shock. How many people knew her in this town?

The woman must have noticed her surprised face. "Your grandma always showed us pictures of you, and was always very proud of you," the woman explained.

Sofia stretched her hand out to her. "It's nice to meet you."

Many of the church members engaged in conversations after the service, and Sofia didn't want to keep Trevor from socializing. She stood close to Trevor as he was greeted by several people. "Who's the beautiful lady?" another woman asked, and Theda took the pleasure of responding.

"Sofia Wise." She smiled mischievously at Trevor. "She's Trevor's friend."

"Wise, as in Jason and Marissa?" another woman asked with a questioning eyebrow, although she gave Sofia a warm embrace that erased any doubts that she was welcome. Sofia received two more hugs from strangers.

Sofia had to admit the Wise family had some kind of reputation, whatever it was, so she decided to keep her mouth shut. Thankfully, they were interrupted by a middle-aged man and a petite, beautiful young lady.

"You must be Sofia. Trevor won't stop yapping about you." The handsome, tall black man smiled.

She grinned at the information as Trevor looked away in embarrassment.

Theda wrapped her in a hug and kissed her cheek. "It was so nice to meet you, young lady." The genuineness in her voice made Sofia feel comfortable.

"Nice to meet you, too, Theda," she said. When Theda had walked away, Sofia turned to the guy who'd just approached.

She stretched out a hand for a handshake, but the man spread his arms out for a hug. Sofia moved closer and hugged him back.

"I'm Trevor's dad, Rex." The man wasn't as tall as Trevor, but he was lean, with salt and pepper hair.

"I've heard a lot about you, too," Sofia said as she left his embrace. She spotted a young black beauty whose features resembled Trevor's standing right next to Rex, and assumed her to be Trevor's sister. "You must be Keisha."

The girl nodded and smiled, waving at her. "Hi. You're just as pretty as he's told us."

"And you're even prettier than he's told me."

"Thank you." Keisha sent Sofia a shy smile. She was adorable with such soft brown eyes. Sofia could see why Trevor spoke so much of her.

"All right, guys, Sofia and I are going to see Pastor Benjamin. Meet you at the house?" Trevor draped a casual arm across her shoulders.

"Sure," they both agreed in unison.

"We look forward to having you join us for lunch," Rex said and patted Sofia's shoulder.

After such a warm introduction, Sofia had no doubt she would have a great time hanging out with Trevor's family.

"I can't wait!" Sofia responded.

Sofia was looking forward to meeting the pastor. She wanted to not only relay to him how impressed she was by his preaching, but to ask a few spiritual questions that she couldn't wait until next Sunday to receive the answers for. Being in Trevor's church had also given Sofia another little glimpse into him. He was like a perfectly wrapped up present she couldn't quite figure out, and every layer she unwrapped showed a little more of his character that made her appreciate the man she was with.

Trevor took her hand and led her to the pastor, who was standing on the opposite side of the sanctuary from them, talking with some members of the congregation. Sofia was aware they had been getting strange stares from the congregation, but she'd blocked it out, mostly because Trevor was next to her. When he was near, she felt as if all the pieces of her past that had shaped her for so long had fallen away. She was practically a new person.

All the people in Trevor's church seemed to know each other, and despite their genuine and welcoming nature, Sofia wondered if she could ever fit in. She could see herself blending amongst the members, whose diversity she appreciated. Her parent's church consisted of a single race, with a few stray members that didn't quite fit the mold, but everyone was wealthy. Here, there was clearly a variety of income levels and ethnicities, yet everyone melded together, getting along just fine.

"Pastor," Trevor said as they approached the older man, pulling Sofia from her thoughts. Thankfully, the pastor had dismissed those he had been talking to before they reached him.

"Trevor, how are you?"

Both men shook hands. "I'm fine, sir. I want you to meet Sofia," Trevor said with an obvious note of excitement in his voice.

Pastor Benjamin turned to her. He was dark with salt and pepper hair, short and stocky, but had a deep, resonating voice.

"So, this is the lovely Miss Wise I've been told of. It's nice to meet you, Miss," Pastor Benjamin said as he stretched his hand for a shake. Sofia wondered how the pastor knew her name when she hadn't bothered to introduce herself, but Trevor had said small town word got around fast. Unless Trevor had already told the pastor himself.

Sofia smiled and accepted the pastor's hand. "Nice to meet you as well, Pastor. Your sermon today was very good."

"Thank you, child. I hope you both took something away from it."

"I definitely did," Sofia said.

"My sermon is only good enough if someone is impacted by it," he stated with a smile.

"I have a few questions, but I'm not sure if now is a good time, or if I should make an appointment."

"Of course." Pastor Benjamin seemed eager as he rummaged in his pockets. "I would leave you my number, but I don't have a piece of paper."

"I have your number, Pastor," Trevor said, his eyes intent on Sofia. "I'll make sure she gets it."

The pastor turned his gaze to Trevor. "Will you do that, please?"

Trevor nodded.

"Oh, by the way," Pastor added. "Benny just sent word that he'll be back in town for a brief visit. He's excited to see you."

Judging from the conversation between the pastor and Trevor, Sofia assumed Benny to be the pastor's son and Trevor's childhood friend who'd left Eron some years ago in search of himself. Apparently, he and Trevor hadn't spoken in a while, ever since Benny had changed his cell number.

"Wow, that's great, I can't wait to catch up," Trevor said.

"Of course, I know you're busy keeping the town safe. Maybe you can put him to work."

Trevor smiled. "Between repainting the station and helping our teens in the community?" Trevor nodded. "There's plenty of work that Benny can help us accomplish."

They said a few final words to the pastor and bid him farewell. "Have a nice day," Trevor said before both men shook hands again, and Pastor Benjamin left them to attend to another person waiting.

"So, ready to head over to lunch?" Sofia asked.

Trevor grinned mischievously. "I hope you're hungry."

"Sofia Wise?"

At the sound of her name, Sofia turned to see her one and only friend from Eron. Walking towards her in graceful strides, her dark skin smooth and vibrant, was a woman dressed in a knee-length dress and designer shoes.

"Chloe Love?"

Trevor stepped aside as Sofia let out a squeal of pleasure at the sight of her old friend. They stretched out their arms to each other for an embrace.

"Oh it's so good to see you, Sofia."

"You, too."

Chloe had the warmest brown eyes Sofia had ever seen. "You look even more beautiful than when you were a teenager," Sofia said after the embrace.

Sofia was glad to know someone else in town besides her own family. She should have reached out to Chloe sooner, but it had been so long since they last spoke, she wasn't sure her friend even had the same number.

Chloe had been Sofia's childhood friend, even though they'd never gone to the same school. They saw each other when both their grandparents would hang out at the Love residence for their knitting night twice a week. Both Sofia and Chloe had joined their grandparents at the Love's house to knit.

"So do you, girlfriend." Chloe's face turned serious. "I'm so sorry for the loss of your grandma," she said, blinking away her tears, which sent a sensation of moisture to Sofia's own eyes. Trevor was still standing by her side and ran a comforting hand over her shoulder. He moved swiftly and returned with a tissue that Sofia took and used to blow her nose.

It was likely Chloe felt responsible for starting a sensitive conversation, so she changed the subject with an attempt at humor.

"Rumor has it that you're dating the town's handsome detective."

Chloe's eyes went to Trevor, whose smile came out more like a grimace.

"I am starting to realize how fast word gets around in this town," Sofia said and then blew her nose again. "I always kept to myself back in the day. I never realized how bad it was."

"Welcome to Eron, girl! If you'd been with the locals long enough you would've known that's how a small town rolls."

"Tell me about it!" Sofia's brow arched in amusement. She stared at her friend and wondered how she could look so stylish in such a tiny town, especially since she hadn't seen anything fancy in the area. Chloe's jet-black skin glowed just like Trevor's, and waves of dark hair flowed to her shoulders.

"Where did you get the designer shoes in such a tiny town? You look amazing!"

"Thanks! I have my personal shoe vendors," Chloe responded. "You don't look shabby yourself."

"Did you stay in Eron this whole time?"

Chloe shook her head. "I'm back from Boston. I came to take care of my mom after her knee surgery and then decided to stay. I just opened a boutique on Main Street two months ago."

Chloe told Sofia about some of her adventures, and Sofia shared about her life, too. A part of Sofia was taken aback by how happy Chloe seemed to be back in the small town they'd both called home.

By the end of their chat, they'd made plans to meet later in the week. After they parted, Sofia was so glad she came to the second service as Trevor had suggested, because seeing Chloe again was like having a special homecoming, and memories of her grandma came flooding back. She never thought of her grandma without thinking of Chloe.

Not only that, but she was sure she felt something stirring inside her. A sense of peace she hadn't felt consistently in years had started to wash over her as the pastor began speaking and reading verses from the Bible. She even considered pulling out her dusty Bible when she got home and reading some verses on her own—she wanted to maintain this peace she was feeling, but she wasn't sure if it was just in her head, or the fact she had seen Chloe again, or even the presence of Trevor. Whatever it was, she knew she needed it.

As Chloe walked away, Sofia and Trevor waved goodbye together.

"Call me," Sofia mouthed as her friend left.

CHAPTER 12

Trevor sat in the safety of his car, contemplating the wisdom in what he was about to do. It was the day of Sofia's grandmother's post-funeral ceremony, and Trevor was parked outside the venue. Of course, it was a family only event and he had no intention on crashing their service.

He figured he could just stand at a distance and provide the support Sofia needed, and perhaps use the excuse of his position as a detective to explain his presence if anyone asked. He could say he was simply there to monitor and keep the peace. Plus, a venue at the cemetery was public land—anybody was welcome, or so he kept telling himself.

He was aware of how much Sofia loved her grandmother. The woman was practically the only person in her family she was truly happy to talk about, and he also knew how much her death had saddened her. It was only fitting that he provide some form of emotional support for her at this time, even if it was from afar. Besides, he knew how much it hurt to lose someone you cared about. He wanted to be there for Sofia, because even though she was coping with it, funerals had a way of stirring up emotions and grief. He only wished he could be standing beside her, holding her hand as she cried.

However, there was something utterly silly about being anywhere close to an event of this magnitude, considering the state of the relationship he had with the rest of her family.

He put his key in the ignition to start the car and drive off, but he couldn't quite do it. What kind of man would he be if he couldn't be there for a girl he'd fallen for when she needed him most? Wasn't there a limit to playing cat and mouse with the Wise family? At some point, he had to make himself known to them, regardless of whatever commotion it might cause.

That's if he and Sofia would take their relationship any further. They would eventually have to tell them they were dating when it came down to it. He couldn't hide from them forever—he was a grown man, and such games were beneath him.

He'd watched the mourners walk out of the building to a gravesite; much closer to the building where they'd had the ceremony. The family had chosen one of the best spots in the cemetery to bury Eunice.

This wasn't a typical cemetery. It had lush green grass and a water fountain in each section, with vibrant flower gardens next to the fountains. There was a magnificent view of the mountains that made you forget for a second that you were at a cemetery.

The cemetery was newly purchased by a wealthy immigrant from Russia who'd thought it would be a perfect investment. Everything the Wise's did was classy and luxurious. Money wasn't a hindrance for them. Trevor wondered what that must be like.

That was another thing about Sofia that had him feeling insecure about their relationship. Trevor knew he worked hard, but being a small town lawman didn't offer a lot of money. Enough to supplement to his dad's butcher income, and save some to build his own house. He'd purchased the land next door to his childhood home from a former neighbor who'd moved out of state.

Unfortunately, sometimes he felt like he wouldn't be able to give Sofia the life she was used to, the life she deserved. No matter how hard he tried, there was always the nagging feeling that he wasn't the kind of man who could give her the things she deserved. He was a working man with an average income, and men like him just didn't get to date women like Sofia Wise. She had never done anything to make him feel inadequate, but Trevor was a proud man, and being with Sofia brought out some of his insecurities, no matter how hard he tried to shove them aside.

He got out of the car and walked toward the family as he maintained a safe distance. Leaning against one of the shaded mature trees, Trevor watched Sofia's family standing around the gravesite. Sofia stood next to her brother. Trevor could tell she was crying by the way she held her head low and blew her nose constantly, yet no one was making an effort to console her. Trevor frowned. How could these people be so cold?

Everybody started walking away, leaving Sofia at the gravesite. Patience wasn't one of Trevor's strongest virtues, and the little he had was dwindling fast. He couldn't stand by silently and watch Sofia cry with no one to comfort her. He drew near enough to see Sofia better, but stopped before he could be seen.

He walked a little closer as if he was going to join Sofia as she stood alone by her grandmother's grave, but stopped when Brent's steely gaze met his.

Rather than turn around and leave, Trevor stood his ground and returned Brent's hard gaze. He watched him whisper something to their father, who turned in his direction. The older man nodded and Brent left the rest of the party to approach Trevor.

Brent took his sunglasses off as he approached him. Meanwhile, Trevor shoved his hands in his pockets to keep his fists hidden. "What do you think you're doing here, Freeman? First our house, now my grandmother's gravesite? We should put a restraining order on you."

Trevor clenched his jaw. "I only came for Sofia," Trevor said evenly. While he didn't like one thing about Brent, for more reasons besides his arrogance, loving Sofia meant he had to at least tolerate her family members more than usual. Besides, they weren't being 'family,' and she needed someone to be there for her.

"You need to stay away from my sister. She may not be making the best decisions in her life right now, as you notice she's vulnerable, but surely, you have the sense to know when you're no more than a liability to someone." He gave a derisive smile. "You and Sofia will never happen."

"Unless you're Sofia, I don't see why your opinion should count," Trevor replied, hiding his own uncertainty.

"I'm her brother, and I know that gold diggers like you don't belong anywhere near a prestigious family like ours. You would do well to remember where you stand in society, to not try reaching for things that are way beyond you." Trevor couldn't come up with a rebuttal for Brent's continued insults, so he could only stare at Brent with a hard gaze while the cocky jerk grinned at him. "Now, if you don't mind, it would be best if you turn around before I call for security."

Trevor felt like reminding Brent that he was security, but he no longer had the will to argue any more.

Once again, Trevor was given a front seat view to Brent's victorious exit. He forced his hands further into his pockets in tight fists that threatened to rip his pants. That was the safest place his hands could be, to keep him from reaching out and beating the man up. If the task were up to him alone, he would see it done, but he had to answer to God for his actions. However, being around Brent made him feel like getting into a fistfight.

Regardless of his cockiness, Brent was right—Trevor had no business being here. Maybe Brent was also right about Sofia as well—she was way beyond his reach.

He walked away from the cemetery with a broken ego and a sense of helplessness. Not only could he not financially provide for Sofia in the way she deserved, but he couldn't even be there for her emotionally in her time of need. He wanted to fight harder for her, but he didn't want to ruin anything, either. If only he was wealthy, or perhaps even braver, he would be standing beside Sofia, holding her hand, squeezing it as she cried.

But instead, she cried alone. And perhaps that's how she needed to mourn, he told himself. Perhaps she needed to go through this alone. And then, as if out of nowhere, a thought came into his mind, *She is not alone for I am with her*.

***

Sofia sat in the reception area of Trevor's office. This is what she had been forced to do after days of not being able to reach him. He hadn't called her in days and he wouldn't pick up her calls or respond to any of her texts. The last time she'd heard from him was on the day of her grandmother's post-funeral, when he had sent a condolence text message. Since then it was like he had fallen off the face of the earth, and she was miserable.

She couldn't think of any reason why he would just cut off all contact from her, so she'd decided to search for him for some answers. Only finding him proved to be almost as difficult as reaching him. He was rarely ever home, and she'd not seen him at church on Sunday, but then, his father Rex Freeman had said he'd had to work that day since his colleague had been sick.

She'd seen Rex a few times, although the old man had failed to disclose Trevor's location, only telling her that he was hurting as much as she was.

Well, that just didn't make sense. If he was hurting half as much as she was, he would have made a conscious effort to find her like she was doing for him. He had her running around the entire town, and for what? She'd hoped to see him after her grandmother's funeral—she needed somebody to talk to. Someone who cared. *But*, her mind whispered, *clearly he doesn't.*

Yet here she was, like one of those desperate women you see on TV, hopelessly clinging to something that doesn't exist … but didn't it? The two had grown so close within the last two months. How could things suddenly be over? Why couldn't he at least have the courtesy to text her back—even if it was just to say he didn't want anything to do with her anymore? She wondered if it had to do with the case against her parents … if he'd finally realized the one thing she had been fearing this entire time—that their relationship might not survive that roadblock.

She paced around the barn office and knocked on the open door to the office that belonged to Scott, the chief of police. The old man arched a brow through his glasses, which were perched precariously at the bottom of his nose.

"What time is he coming back?" Sofia asked.

"Hard to tell, but he should be back soon. Help yourself to some soda from the fridge."

Sofia glanced at the small fridge in the waiting area and wrinkled her nose. "I'm good, thanks, Scott. "

She took a few seconds to study the spacious interior; there was a long dark corridor straight ahead, she hadn't toured that side of the building yet, but Trevor had told her there were three rooms at the end of the corridor where criminals were temporarily placed before they were moved to the county jail. One of the rooms held the juvenile, one for women and the third room was for the male prisoners.

She fanned herself with her hand, as her hair and shirt dampened. She moved to a closed window and stared at the blazing sun.

Realizing she couldn't wait in the hot farmhouse any longer, and sitting outside was not something she wanted to do while her mind whirled with several questions about Trevor, Sofia stepped outside and walked to the parking lot. The sound a of car door slamming caused her to look up, and sure enough, there was the evasive Trevor Freeman, marching towards the office, oblivious to his surrounding that he didn't even see her

Sofia cleared her throat to announce her presence.

When his gaze met hers, his body tensed and his expression turned stern and serious—the perfect detective face. He looked at her as if she was a criminal he was about to arrest.

Looking closer, she could tell he looked more contrite than hostile. He also looked very much exhausted, his eyes red and ringed in dark circles.

After all, he was the architect of his own problems.

"Can we talk?" she asked, realizing she was going to have to initiate the conversation.

"Sure." He turned to walk towards the building and Sofia followed him.

They ended up in a room that was occupied by a desk and a table piled with lots of papers. She could tell it was Trevor's office by the two framed pictures on his desk. One was a family picture with a teenaged Trevor in it, and a woman Sofia guessed to be his mom. The other picture was of Trevor and his little sister playing in a lake. She took a seat on one of the chairs and looked over at him. "Your mom is beautiful."

Trevor leaned against the end of the table with his hands crossed over his chest. He was silent long enough for Sofia to assume he was not going to respond.

"That's what we all think," he finally spoke.

They shared a long stare for almost another minute, although it seemed like an hour to Sofia, and neither of them uttered a word. Just when Sofia was going to break the silence, he did instead. "You look good," he began.

"You look terrible."

A sour smile came upon his lips. "Yeah, so I've been told."

"I suppose you owe me an explanation," she stated, then waited for a response. However, he failed to get straight to the point.

"How have you been?" Trevor asked.

"Fine, not that you cared to check."

He nodded. "I'm sorry about that, Sofia."

"I don't need you to be sorry, I need you to tell me why you've been avoiding me," she stated firmly, though she couldn't keep the hint of desperation from her voice.

He looked down at his feet, and then at her face. "I was at the cemetery the day you had your grandmother's post-funeral," he stated plainly. While the information surprised her because she hadn't noticed him there, Sofia ensured her face remained stoic as he continued. "I wanted to support you, so I went to the cemetery. I didn't get to see you, but Brent came up to me and ..." Trevor trailed off. He ran a hand through his hair. "He told me some things I couldn't deny, some things I had been feeling, but had refused to acknowledge."

Of course Brent would be involved in whatever had caused her to be unhappy. "Things like what?"

He looked down at his feet once again. What was so interesting about those tacky shoes he had on? He sighed and looked up at her. "Sofia, I...I'm not good enough for you."

She raised a brow. "Meaning?"

"I'm not the kind of guy you should be with. I'm not in your class, and will never be." He shrugged and turned to stare at the window. "I can't give you the things you need, and the life you deserve ..."

Sofia had feared that their world might come undone because of his mom's case, and family heat, but she'd never expected him to use money as a hindrance factor to their relationship.

"I can't believe you're saying this to me, Trevor!" She rose from her seat and moved closer to face him. "Have I ever made demands of you that you couldn't fulfill? Have I ever given you the impression that I'm interested in money?"

"It's not you Sofia. It's me. I'm the one with the insecurities."

She couldn't help her scoff. "Obviously. Is that why you've been avoiding me?"

Now he looked at her and ran a hand over his face. "I can't be the man you need me to be Sofia. I love you, but … this war between me and your family, it takes a lot out of our relationship. I don't want to be the outcast in your family. I don't want you to become the black sheep. If we're going to be together, it can't be with all this hate and insecurities. I … I can't do this anymore."

Sofia hadn't been aware she had tears in her eyes until the first drop fell at those words. She wiped it defiantly, but it didn't lessen the pain in her soul. She poked at his chest, her voice cracking. "Well, you should've thought about all that before making me fall for you." She picked up her bag from the table and made her way out of the office.

So much for the good feelings, she had felt when she got off the plane over seven weeks ago. All Colorado had for her was pain and hurt. It was all it had ever given her.

She didn't feel like going home, where everyone was into themselves, so she called Chloe, who answered the phone right away.

"Sweetie, you don't sound good," Chloe spoke through the phone. All Sofia could manage was to blow her nose.

"Come to the boutique. I'm not busy this time of day," Chloe said and hung up.

It didn't take long for Sofia to make it to the end of Main Street, where Chloe's boutique was located. She'd come to Chloe's boutique a few times, so that had made it much easier to navigate her way to the place without having to read each door sign.

Chloe embraced her as she walked into the shop. "Come have a seat." She led Sofia to one of the three bold red sofa chairs she'd set up in one corner of her shop and handed Sofia a box of tissues.

"Let's not talk about anything for a few minutes," Chloe suggested, placing a water bottle from a small refrigerator onto the small table in front of Sofia. She explained that she kept the refrigerator because she needed to be prepared in case she was snowed in and had to stay the night in her boutique.

"Hey, Carl," Chloe called over her shoulder to the young teenage boy who helped her in the shop during his summer break. "Can you please go get us some ice cream from Theda's?" She told the boy what flavors to bring, then turned to face Sofia. "Comfort food helps. Trust me." Chloe placed a hand of comfort on her friend's shoulder.

Sofia took a deep breath and blew her nose again. "Can you believe that Trevor broke up with me?"

Chloe's mouth dropped open. "It's not about the case with his mom, is it?"

"A little of that, but his main excuse was that he couldn't offer me the things I needed."

Just saying the words "break up" created a new set of tears from Sofia.

"The worst part is that I still love him and I feel like this whole thing is not over yet," she spoke in a shaky voice. "Is that crazy?"

Chloe shook her head meditatively. "First, you're not crazy, and second, I can't believe that Trevor used money as an excuse to break up with you. I thought he was tougher than that. He fell for you regardless of whatever issues he had with your family."

That was the same question Sofia was wondering about, too. "I can't change the fact that my family has money, or that they're not the easiest people to be around."

"Well," Chloe said, face serious. "He better come to his senses soon enough to realize that he made a mistake in letting you go before I place him in a category of my own."

Sofia had no idea what Chloe meant by category, but she hoped Trevor would call her soon, too. She missed him already, yet she had to get back to New York at some point. "I don't have time to wait for him to come around. I'm leaving soon."

Sofia knew that the reason for her visit, her grandma's funeral, was over. For a while, she was almost tempted to change her mind and stay. Her family hadn't changed very much except that she and her dad had made some progress in their relationship. They could talk, but her dating Trevor had brought a little tension.

Maybe her leaving was for the best, she mused. Besides, when she'd just arrived in Eron, she'd never planned on staying. Their relationship was still new—wouldn't it be unwise to leave her life behind for some guy who practically thought of her family as a bunch of murderers?

"I don't have much relationship advice to offer," Chloe spoke sincerely. "But all I can say is I would love for you to stay. I miss my friends. Jules left and never looked back." Jules was Sofia's cousin whose mom was always on the move. Jules's mom and stepdad hadn't been as uptight as Marissa about their daughter hanging out with the community people, so Jules had made a few friends. She'd ended up being Chloe's best friend.

"Do you still keep in touch with Jules?" Sofia felt like talking about anything else but Trevor.

"Yes, and she wants to come back to Eron," she said. "Once she heard I returned, she's been talking more about returning."

"I wish I could stay."

They chatted until Carl returned with the ice cream. The girls dug into their ice cream and talked about all sorts of things, including their childhood memories of baking cookies while their grandmother's knitted together, and gossiping.

"Remember that time you took me to that store?" Sofia asked, scooping up a spoonful of soft vanilla ice cream.

"Oh, yeah, and when your mom found out about the soaps you'd bought, she threw them in the trash and you got all mad at her."

Sofia laughed at the bitter memory. That had been the beginning of her desire to get away from her family for a while, Warren's attack had been the last straw. She'd ended up moving to New York and living with her aunt for her high school years.

"I am trying to forgive my family," she said softly while Chloe shoveled another spoonful of ice cream into her mouth.

The shop wasn't busy during this time of day, which allowed them to talk freely.

Chloe turned to face Sofia again and held her hands. "Let me pray with you before you leave," she said. "Heavenly Father, God of the universe, you know everything about us, when we sleep and when we wake up. I pray that you will give Sofia peace that only comes from you. You brought her and Trevor together for a reason. I pray that you will fulfill your purpose for their relationship." She said a few more closing prayers before they both said in unison, "Amen."

"Try to remember this verse in Matthew 6:33 Seek first the kingdom of God and the rest will be added unto you," Chloe said. "Let God take care of Trevor and all the details will work out." She let go of Sofia's hands.

Sofia had had a good conversation with the pastor, although she'd not yet made that commitment to Christ, and she knew what she needed to do. She already felt a sense of peace fill her chest, warming and comforting her entire body as her friend prayed on her behalf. Yet she still found herself feeling hesitant about making a commitment to Christ. It wasn't that she didn't believe, she just felt like she wasn't worthy, and for a moment a thought came into her mind, one she pushed down because it felt too real, as if God himself was speaking it to her—*That's how Trevor feels.*

Sofia rose from her seat. "Thanks so much for listening and praying with me."

Chloe embraced her. "Call or text anytime when you get to New York, and come back to visit soon this time, will you?"

Sofia nodded as she exited the boutique feeling hopeful, having been reminded that she was in God's care. She found herself hoping to know more about God than wanting to chase her own dreams, because that didn't seem to get her anywhere. She knew how she'd felt in church—she knew that was the part of life that mattered. She had seen what success could do to people. She thought there was nothing wrong with success in itself, but it did not bring joy without Christ.

She thought of her family and the dreams they chased. Those dreams often weren't aligned with God's will, she knew that. She saw their greed and how they felt like they were above others. Sofia knew she wanted to be humble and kind. She wanted to be someone God would look upon and smile ... and she wanted that with her whole heart.

CHAPTER 13

Trevor walked around his father's house like a lifeless robot. He pulled his cell phone from the pocket of his sweats, taking another cursory glance at the blank screen for the nineteenth time over the last two weeks, as if he expected a call or text from Sofia. He knew she wasn't going to call, but that didn't stop him from missing her. He paced the room, unbearably restless, frustrated, and helpless.

It was exactly how he'd felt ever since he'd broken off things with Sofia. It had become worse after he'd found out from Chloe that Sofia had left town. She hadn't even said goodbye, but then why would she, since he'd chased her away? Just imagining their last conversation when he'd seen a teardrop fall from her eyes—tears that he'd caused—had been painfully piercing. It had taken every ounce of discipline in him to not wrap himself around her and tell her how much he loved her.

She loved him, she'd said it herself that day, yet he'd still thrown words of rejection at her. He thumped his head on the wall a couple of times as he continued replaying his last conversation with her.

He'd considered taking some time off from work so he could go find Sofia in New York, because a phone call was not enough to fix the mess he'd put himself into. But being one of the only three law enforcement agents in town, he couldn't punish his colleagues by taking a whole week off so he could fix his personal life that he'd so willingly thrown down the drain.

The pounding on the door caused him to turn, but he dismissed it and stared through the window where he could watch his unfinished house from a distance. He'd started picturing himself and Sofia in that house someday, but there was no sense in torturing himself with a dream he'd already lost.

"Hi, Enrique!" Keisha's soft voice sounded and Trevor turned to stare at the door.

"Hey, Keisha." Enrique pecked Keisha on both cheeks, something he did with every woman he knew, including his mom. It was either hand kisses or pecks for greeting.

"Trevor's not up to having company today," Keisha said.

Enrique dodged his way past Keisha to let himself in the house. "I'm not company," he said, and his gaze met Trevor's instantly where he was standing by the window since their living room was the first room after an entry hallway.

"Dude, you don't stand me up for two days in a row," Enrique spoke, moving his fingers. "We gotta go run because when we're chasing a criminal, I'm not going to be throwing balls at a wall to bring down the bad guy."

In case Enrique didn't get the message that Trevor was in no mood for socializing, Trevor made an effort to send his colleague a steely gaze, only to realize that the Italian guy was not the one to back off easily when he took two steps closer and inched into Trevor's personal space. Enrique put both hands on his hips and narrowed his gaze at Trevor. "I'm afraid to say that you're coming with me. You promised to be my running mate, and you can't back out now."

Trevor ground his teeth. He'd skipped their morning run yesterday, and had told Enrique he wasn't up to it today either.

It wasn't even funny how much longer the days seemed to drag on than he'd remembered. He wondered what life had been like before Sofia, but he'd forgotten the fact that Sofia had come with a wave of happiness that had changed his life for the last three months.

He'd been working a case with the DA's office, helping them with a criminal gang case involving one of the popular gangs in El Paso County called the Black Eagles.

If he wasn't working, he was keeping up with all the seniors and single parents who needed a little extra help with raking leaves or minor home improvement projects. Otherwise, he just sat at home lost in his thoughts, and for the first time, he had no desire to eat. He supposed he should be grateful to his colleague Enrique, who'd still dragged him to go for their regular run, giving him something else to do than wallow.

Besides, he needed to stay in shape for times when he needed to chase or muscle down a strong criminal. If he'd known falling in love would bring him so much pain, he would never have gone after Sofia.

Enrique pointed a finger at him. "I won't ask what you're plotting in your mind, but I know that you don't leave for work for another hour and a half," Enrique said, staring at his watch. "You should be back by seven thirty. Plus, you will thank me for keeping you in shape when the pretty lady returns." He turned his back to Trevor. "I will be waiting by the front door."

Good thing Trevor was still in his sweats, not as fancy as Enriques' running suit, but it would have to do. Trevor gave a resigned sigh and scrubbed a hand down his face. Seemed he was going for a run after all.

***

The next day, Trevor went to church with his family. The pastor was teaching about forgiveness, using the passage where Peter asked Jesus how many times he should forgive someone who had wronged him. Then the pastor quoted Jesus' response from Matthew 18:21-22 ... *Jesus answered, "I tell you, not seven times, but seventy times seven times."*

"Forgive, because hate is just another way of holding on, and you don't belong there anymore," the pastor said, then continued with the sermon as Trevor's heart sank with each word that seemed aimed directly at him.

God sure had a way of using evangelists to reach the right people. "Holding onto anger is like holding onto an anchor and jumping into the sea. If you don't let it go, you will drown." The pastor's words created another rush of heat through Trevor. He clasped his fingers tightly together and couldn't stop thinking about how much he'd felt for the last few years, holding onto the past, yet God alone controlled the past, present, and future. The bitterness he'd allowed to build up towards the Wise family felt like lead in his stomach.

His heart felt heavy when he left the church that day battling with conviction. That afternoon, after their family lunch, he went to his special place by the creek, where he re-visited Matthew 18:21-22 and reflected on Pastor's message from earlier. The words kept ringing in his mind, "If you don't let go, you will drown."

He was drowning in sin, bitterness, and anger.

That night in his room, he knelt on the floor and leaned his elbows on the bed, then bowed his head over his clasped hands. After asking God for forgiveness, he prayed for Sofia to be saved. She was too sweet to miss out on knowing Christ. And maybe that was why God had split them apart in the first place—they had different beliefs. Sofia wasn't a believer, even though she'd been more of a saint than Trevor had, trusting a guy like him who had a beef with her family. She'd seen above all the hatred and still confided in him. More than that, she'd offered her love to Trevor no matter the difference in their social status and family tension.

Sofia knew her family was not the best, yet she was trying harder to connect with them. She definitely had more faith than Trevor had ever had.

Trevor ran both hands over his face, his heart heavy. Shaking, he sprawled on the floor, sobbing, tears streaming down his face—something he'd never done in his adult life. "Oh God, what a wretched sinner I am. Forgive me, Father, for letting you down. What kind of witness have I been to the Wise family who don't know You?"

Trevor considered himself a Christian, yet he'd done a terrible job representing Christ to the Wise family. What if he was the closest person to Christ Brent had ever been around?

He sobbed in his prayers, "God, will You please give me another chance with the Wise family, to prove to them that You've transformed me?"

Trevor had been upset at first that his dad didn't seem too worked up about Jayla's disappearance, but now he was starting to realize that Rex had surrendered all to God.

And that's exactly what Trevor needed to do. He felt his heart relax as a feeling of comfort swept over him. He reached for his Bible from the nightstand and sat on the carpeted floor, flipping the pages, until he landed on Romans 12:19. *"Beloved, never avenge yourselves, but leave it to the wrath of God, for it is written, "Vengeance is mine, I will repay, says the Lord."*

Letting those words sink in, Trevor knew without a doubt that first thing tomorrow morning, he was calling his lawyer to drop the charges, and then making the dreaded drive to the Wise family and apologize for all the time he'd spent harassing them.

Rose Fresquez

Whether his mom was dead or still alive, Trevor had to let God take over. How was God supposed to do the work, since Trevor had been in God's way for the last six years?

He closed his eyes, basking in an abundant peace that he hadn't experienced in such a long time. He knew that everything was going to be okay. Whether he and Sofia ever happened or not, he was still in God's care.

***

Sofia had no idea why she was back in Eron, but for the first time in a long time, she wanted to be home for the holidays. Something incredible had happened two weeks ago that made her see things differently—she'd given her life to Christ.

Sitting in her apartment in New York, she'd been flipping through the channels on her television and happened to land on a Christian program. The preacher had taught with a passion that reminded her of Pastor Benjamin in Eron.

At the end of his sermon, the pastor had extended an invitation for listeners to receive Christ. "There might be someone who's been wanting to make this decision for quite some time, but whenever you try, you get cold feet. Today is the day of salvation, don't wait for tomorrow, because you may not have tomorrow. Today is all you've got."

Sofia's stomach had knotted up, and there was a strange stirring in her heart. For some reason, she'd felt like the pastor had been talking directly to her, and an irresistible longing rose up in her to pray along with him.

After the prayer, the TV pastor had said that the first step for those who'd accepted Christ was to share the news with someone, and the second step was to find a Bible-teaching church to connect with other believers.

Sofia had called her former roommate Mandy, and she'd suggested a good church in the area. The second person that came to mind had been Chloe, who'd rejoiced with Sofia over the phone and mailed her a bunch of Christian literature to go along with the Bible.

As much as she'd wanted to call and talk to Trevor, she'd not had the courage to do so. She'd been hoping he would call and say he'd been kidding about the break-up, but that hadn't been the case.

Sofia yawned, wishing it wasn't too late in the day for her to drink caffeine. She was still on New York time, since she'd just arrived yesterday, but she couldn't wait to see Chloe. As she drove along past the quiet streets that afternoon, the leaves rustled, falling on her windshield as she wiped them off. Every now and then, she passed a few people raking leaves. Regardless of what happened between her and Trevor, for the first time, Sofia felt Eron was home.

She still had Grandma's house that she'd left for both Sofia and Brent. Sofia doubted Brent wanted anything to do with the small house. It was very old and would probably need to be demolished. But she didn't have it in her heart to sell it. It was the only connection she had left to her grandmother. She would just buy out Brent's share and keep the property for herself.

She came to the end of the row of shops and parked in front of Chloe's boutique. As usual, they exchanged squeals, embracing and ending up on the comfy sofas in the shop.

"Can I get you anything to drink?" Chloe offered.

"Water is perfect."

Chloe stopped to exchange greetings with one of the two customers browsing in the shop, while her helper, Carl, was fixing clothes on and off the racks. She returned with Sofia's water bottle and sat across from her. "I want to hear more about your salvation experience."

Sofia beamed, sitting up straighter. She shared her story again, telling her about the church she'd visited in New York. She'd never felt this much joy before. She'd enjoyed having Trevor in her life, but this joy came with the assurance that no matter what circumstance came her way, God would still be with her. That was a unique kind of joy.

"Isn't that what God does for us?" Chloe spoke. "How long are you staying this time?"

"I'm here for three weeks. I will have two extra weeks after Thanksgiving to catch up with the family, and with you, of course," Sofia said. She also intended to fix up her grandma's house during the three weeks, and then go back to New York for the rest of the year before she made plans to return. She didn't want to share that part with Chloe just yet, in case things fell through.

Chloe crossed her legs. "Gosh, that will give us a good amount of time to catch up."

"I look forward to it, too," Sofia said and twisted open her water bottle.

"Speaking of Thanksgiving," Chloe said. "Are you coming to the Thanksgiving dinner put on by the police and firefighters?"

Brent had told Sofia all about the annual dinner that the firefighters and police organized as a way to thank their donors and volunteers. Sofia's family had never gone in the past, but Louis, their chef, had represented them in past years.

This year, her father had announced that they were all going together as a family. It seemed to be Jason's way of welcoming Sofia home. Or at least, he seemed to assume that she was home if she planned to visit Eron every once in a while.

"Actually, my family is going." Her hand flew to her mouth as a realization hit her, and her stomach tied in knots. "I bet Trevor will be there."

"Oh, honey." Chloe crossed her legs. "The whole town comes to these things. And there's no doubt about Trevor being there since it's the police and firefighters who put on the dinner." Chloe curled an eyebrow. "Most of the time Trevor gives the toast. Either him or their chief, Scott."

That news was a bit alarming to Sofia. How was she going to sit and listen to Trevor talk without staring at him? She leaned back in the chair to process this new information.

"Let's get you a dress," Chloe suggested, grabbing Sofia's arm to drag her toward a rack of designer dresses.

Sofia hung back, uncertain. "Uh ... uh, I don't know about getting a dress."

Chloe turned and faced Sofia. "When was the last time you dressed up for something other than a wedding?"

Sofia put two fingers on her lips, trying to remember. It had been a long time since she'd worn a formal dress and a very long time since she'd been at a wedding, too. She'd always dressed professionally for her job, but nothing nearly as fancy as the dresses Chloe was rifling through on the rack.

Chloe held up a red fashionable dress. "This is my most recent creation. Try it on."

Sofia's eyes widened. "You designed this dress? You are so talented."

Chloe nodded. "Thanks!"

There was no way Sofia was leaving without trying on the dress that had been designed by her friend. She left for the dressing room, and returned a few minutes later, draped in a flowing red evening dress with a modest slit on the side. The sequin embellishment added a festive touch.

Chloe gave a nod of approval. "That's the one. Consider it an early Christmas gift from me."

Sofia had looked through the mirror in the dressing room and knew she looked stunning. The dress fit perfect as if it were designed specifically for her. She let out a long breath.

"Okay, I want it," she said when she was out of the dressing room. "It's both non-revealing and classy enough."

Sofia shrugged, her face downcast. "I don't know about wearing this to a community Thanksgiving dinner, though."

Chloe sent her a dubious look. "Now you're just making things hard on yourself."

Sofia's heart was a big problem, but finding something to wear for a fundraiser where Trevor might show was a big deal. Things were over between them, so she had no idea why she was even worried about impressing Trevor. No matter what she tried to tell herself, she couldn't convince her heart that this thing between them was over.

Sofia knew that her feelings for Trevor ran deeper than mere attraction, and she thought Trevor knew it, too. Even though she still wanted something more to happen between them, Trevor wasn't interested. That meant her feelings were her own issues, and she'd just have to figure out how to deal with them.

"Okay, I will take the dress." She sighed in resignation, telling herself it was just a dinner with her family.

After Choe had put Sofia's dress in a fancy tote bag, they said their goodbyes, and that they hoped to see each other at tomorrow's dinner.

Sofia left the boutique in a much better mood, looking forward to sharing Thanksgiving dinner with the people in the community.

***

The afternoon brought a crisp breeze that sent the last leaves fluttering from the colorful aspens in waves. The cool weather was just the perfect match to Trevor's gloomy mood as he stared over the mountain horizon.

Sleep had been a challenge for him lately. If he wasn't worried about his personal life, he'd been bombarded by the images from the videos that he'd been watching for the case that he'd been assigned to by the DA's office. He'd watched some of the gang members' previous crimes from break-ins that had been captured by surveillance cameras, and the images had him worked up. To combat the sluggishness caused by his sleepless nights, Trevor had kicked up his daily caffeine intake, but it hadn't helped—he still walked around in a daze.

He turned to trudge back to the house and noticed his dad headed towards him from the back porch. Rex was carrying two fishing poles and a fishing kit.

"I noticed you standing out here, and thought you would be up for fishing," Rex said when he reached Trevor.

Trevor gritted his teeth and ran a hand through his hair. "It's getting cold."

His dad's face went from smiling to blank, causing Trevor to feel guilty. He and Keisha fished with their dad from time to time, but they hadn't done that all summer long. "Okay, let me just get my coat."

As he turned towards the house, his cell phone rang and he pulled it out of his pocket. His eyes went to the screen and his brows furrowed. "Sorry, Dad, I need to take this."

It was his friend, Detective Dan Reading. Although Dan was two years older than Trevor, they'd grown up in the same neighborhood and had gone to school together until Dan moved to Colorado Springs and joined the police force. He now worked there as a Missing Persons' Investigator.

Trevor knew that Dan was an excellent detective. He'd cracked several difficult cases, which was why Trevor had requested his help in tracking down his mom. He also knew that Dan wouldn't be calling to make small talk.

He cleared his throat so his voice wouldn't shake when he answered the call. "Dan."

"I've got some news for you," Dan said. "Maybe you should sit down."

"Just tell me." Trevor was so intent on hearing Dan's next words that everything around him faded into the distance. His body went hot, then cold, and he trembled so hard he had to use both hands to hold the phone to his ear so he wouldn't drop it.

Dan sighed before dropping the bombshell. "Well, your mom is alive."

Those words left Trevor's mouth hanging open. His stomach dropped and knotted up. That wasn't what he'd been expecting to hear.

Unable to speak, he paced around the small house, still holding the phone against his ear. He ran a hand through his hair, trying to process the information. He'd spent all these years searching for his mother, and now that he knew she was alive, he had no idea whether to be happy or not. If Jayla was alive, where was she? Why hadn't she called his dad or at least her son?

"Are you still there?" Dan finally asked on the other end.

"Yes," Trevor whispered, still unable to make sense of the news.

"There's more," Dan warned. "Are you ready to hear it?"

"Yes," Trevor said again, forcing his voice to sound stronger even though he dreaded what might be coming next.

Dan continued to speak. "Remember that picture I sent five years ago of your mom in a bar with a guy we thought to be Jason Wise? As it turns out, it's actually a very different man."

Trevor's legs wouldn't support him anymore, and he dropped into a chair, thankful that his sister was hanging out at a friend's house and his dad was out fishing.

"And listen to this, my friend." Dan gave another long sigh, pausing before delivering what Trevor assumed would be the piece of information that would send his heart to stroke level. "She also has a six-year-old son."

Trevor did the obvious math. His mother must have been pregnant already when she disappeared. His feelings of betrayal nearly choked him.

By the time Trevor hung up the phone, he was physically and emotionally drained. He took a bitterly cold shower, hoping to numb his own reaction to the devastating revelation. He needed to compose himself before facing his dad. How could he present such shattering news to a man who'd mourned for his wife, a man who'd waited, holding on to the belief that if his wife was somehow still alive, she would return home soon?

Trevor rehearsed the words in his mind. *Oh, by the way, Dad, Mom didn't die, but she just didn't want to be our mother anymore.*

Had Rex suspected all along that Jayla was not dead? Is that why he'd never shared Trevor's bitterness toward the Wises?

***

Sofia checked her reflection in the mirror in the living room one last time, preparing to tag along with her brother on their way to the dinner.

She sipped her water and took a deep breath. Seeing Trevor was going to be much harder than she was ready for, but she still wanted to see his face anyway. Maybe that would remind her that she'd made a mistake by falling in love with the guy.

Perhaps she was drawn to punishment. She liked being tortured, that could be the only reasonable explanation as to why she had decided to come to Colorado for Thanksgiving. She told herself it was because she wanted to reconnect with her family.

In the mirror's reflection, Sofia could see Brent standing right behind her, grinning. "You look drop dead gorgeous, Sofie," he said. "You're going to give the local guys heart attacks."

Sofia did not intend to give anyone a heart attack—the only guy she wanted to notice her was Trevor Freeman but he didn't feel the same way about her.

"Nobody is having a heart attack, Brent." She lifted her hand, waving her brother off.

"Is Mallory coming?" she asked.

"No, it's not her kind of crowd."

Sofia rolled her eyes. Of course, it wasn't Mallory's kind of crowd, but she could at least come and be with her boyfriend. She decided to not voice any of her concerns to Brent. Good thing Mallory knew that her boyfriend wasn't the friendly type unless it served a purpose for his business. Brent was attractive enough to be the cover model for a magazine. Thankfully, this was an event with more locals than the upper class. Sofia doubted any of the girls there who might approach Brent would be his type of girl anyway.

"Oh, by the way." Brent gave a sly smile. "I forgot to tell you that Freeman dropped the charges."

Sofia's small purse tumbled to the floor at the mention of Trevor's last name.

"Are you okay?" Brent asked and stepped aside to let Sofia pick her bag up.

Sofia nodded vaguely.

"Anyway, he came over and apologized. Can you believe it?" Brent shook his head. "And he considers himself a detective. What a loser! I'm so glad you walked out of that relationship. Can you imagine the mess you would be in?"

Sofia's green eyes flashed with anger. Just because she wasn't seeing him anymore, Brent had no right to throw venomous words at Trevor.

"You know, Brent," she sneered, her face icy cold as the air around her. "You are the loser. I will not stand here and listen to you slander a man who has more integrity than you do." Her jaw tightened. "I can expect mom or dad to say that, but not my brother. You never liked him from the start anyway. You people in this family! When are we ever going to be a normal family?"

Brent opened his mouth to respond, then shut it again, looking resigned as if waiting for the rest of what Sofia had to say.

Sofia turned to leave but stopped herself, knowing she shouldn't be fighting with her brother, not if she wanted to reconcile with him and the rest of her family. Turning to him, she studied his face, hating to see how pale it'd turned. Maybe he wanted to reconnect with her just as much.

"Listen," she said in a calm tone. "I love you, and the last thing I need is to argue with you right now. I appreciate the fact that you were bold enough to stand up for me against Warren when Dad and mom didn't." She moved closer to her brother and touched his shoulder.

"I love Trevor." She swallowed. "At least I did—and although it's over between us, the last thing I need to hear you say is anything negative about him to my face. Regardless of your differences, he's a good man who's just trying to find his mother." She closed her eyes and then opened them. "Sometimes people do outrageous things to fight for the ones they love." She wished Trevor had loved her enough to fight for her. "Just like you did for me," she whispered.

Her brother chose silence and turned to kiss her forehead. "Let's get going," he said, and Sofia adjusted the slit on her dress before heading for the door behind him.

The community Thanksgiving dinner was held at a recreation center. Sofia had purposefully decided against wearing a jacket over her dress, so as not to ruin her attire. Keeping one hand to her body, she held the door open for Brent to walk in, and for an elderly couple who followed Brent. The seniors smiled and nodded their thanks.

Another gentleman rushed forward and grabbed the door to hold it open for Sofia. "Ladies first." Sofia sneaked a quick glance toward Brent to see his reaction to the gentleman's statement, but he had already disappeared in the crowd.

"Thank you," she told the gentleman who held the door.

An assortment of pumpkins and gourds decorated the entrance, giving the building a festive look. Strands of lights sparkled above several tables draped in brown linen tablecloths. Some of the tables were still vacant, but most were already occupied by people she recognized from the community. Several people stood around in groups, talking to each other.

Sofia took a deep breath and the scent of cinnamon and homemade food filled her senses. Just like the scent her grandma's house had held. A sense of warmth swept over her, and she knew she was finally home.

Sofia could see her mom and Brent engaged in a conversation near the dessert table. Her dad walked towards her and took her hand.

As she walked with her dad to their table, and even though the last person she wanted to see was Trevor Freeman, she couldn't stop herself from scanning the crowd looking for him.

She'd convinced Brent that she was done with Trevor and she never wanted to see him again, but those words held no weight. The lies in them, though, were heavy. She hadn't gotten over Trevor Freeman, because he was all she saw whenever she closed her eyes at night.

She had returned to New York and done what she usually did to forget her problems—buried herself in work. But even that hadn't been effective. She still thought about him every day, and what could have been. It was pathetic, but she couldn't help it. The man had stolen her heart. Thankfully, her newfound faith in Christ had kept her from losing hope.

She sat at the designated table with her family, trying to participate in their conversation, even though her gaze kept straying to the entrance. After several people entered with no sign of Trevor, Sofia leaned back in her chair, thankful her family hadn't noticed her distraction. They were busy discussing her mom's salon, and who to hire to manage the salon.

Just when Sofia started to relax, the door came open and the Freeman family made their entrance. First came Rex Freeman, who had Keisha walking beside him. Then, the man she had been waiting for.

Sofia felt her breath seize as she finally laid eyes on Trevor. He looked different, his face thin and slightly pale. She didn't have to look underneath his sports coat, the same one he'd worn for their date, to know that he kept a gun strapped to his hip. Had he lost weight on her account? His face didn't have the brightness she was used to seeing. Even that confidence that had attracted her to him didn't seem evident at the moment as he spoke to another gentleman who'd greeted him cheerfully.

Trevor rubbed his hands together and blew a breath on them as if to warm them. The guy still looked as handsome as ever.

Sofia's eyes followed his every step, and when he turned her way, his eyes landed on her and their gazes locked.

There was a brief flash of emotions on his face—surprise, regret, and hope. That last one was the one that killed her and forced her to look away from him. He had no right to look at her like that, looking like he'd missed her. Not after everything he had done. With her stuttering heart, Sofia realized that the next two hours of the event were going to be the longest hours of her life.

Now that Trevor had dropped the charges against her family, she wanted to know what had happened to his mom. Had he found out she was already dead?

Her eyes misty, she turned her gaze back to the family before her, only to find her dad staring at her.

He nodded, but thankfully didn't ask anything. Sofia had no idea what she would say to her dad if he'd asked whether she were okay, because the truth was, she was not okay. She deserved to be punished, because she'd deliberately shown up at the community event, and she could think of no worse punishment than having to see the man who had broken her heart.

CHAPTER 14

Trevor was in no mood to smile at all tonight, but he'd come for two reasons. First, to spend time with his dad and sister, since the news they'd received yesterday had created a thick cloud in their house. Second, he had to be here regardless, since the point of the dinner was to raise money for the police and firefighters.

This was the fourth Annual Thanksgiving Appreciation Dinner, which took place a few days before Thanksgiving. Food had been donated by Ricci's Bistro, except for the turkeys, which had been prepared by another diner in town. The townspeople supplied homemade desserts and sides, and Trevor could smell pies and cobblers the moment he walked in the door. Since he'd had to work today, he'd gotten there late, and it looked like almost everyone in town had shown up before him. Any occasion that offered food, especially for free, pretty much guaranteed that the entire town would be present.

Trevor had expected the room to be filled with a sea of people, all dressed up. What Trevor hadn't planned on today was seeing Sofia Wise. Even in the crowd, she stood out, and seeing her created all sorts of things to happen to his belly. His breathing quickened and his heart lurched, as he felt the urge to head to her table instead of joining his own family. The Wise's had never shown up for the event in the past.

"Our table is over there," Keisha announced, pulling Trevor out of his daze.

Dinner was served by a few volunteers, including his sister, who'd offered to help play waitress. Tables had been set so each family could sit together. People chatted as they ate.

While everyone else enjoyed their food, Trevor's tummy was filled with butterflies. More so because he had caught Sofia's intense gaze on him from time to time, and he was expected to give a toast. He'd done this two times out of the four dinners they'd given, and had never felt this nervous before.

Thankfully, a firefighter was called on to give a toast first. Trevor tried to listen, but none of the firefighter's words registered until the last words of the toast. Lifting his sparkling cider high, the firefighter said, "To Eron."

The rest of the people lifted their glasses in response. "To Eron."

Trevor made his way to the microphone and decided that if his words were going to make any sense, he'd best keep his eyes off Sofia.

"I just want to thank all the faithful volunteers who made this event possible." As he spoke, he fixed his gaze on an empty chair in the very back row.

"Thanks to all our generous donors, who believe in Eron enough to invest in it." He mentioned the names of the families, and his concentration tactic would have still worked, if only he were in control of his eyes. "A huge thank you to the Wise Family." His gaze locked with Sofia's once more, and his words died on his lips. He trailed off and ended with a nod. "To

Eron." He lifted the sparkling cider in the thin tall glass, and everybody in the audience raised their cheers.

"To Eron."

While people clapped, Trevor handed the microphone to the MC and made his way back to his seat, hoping he hadn't made a fool of himself in front of the whole town with a thrown-together toast. He hoped nobody had noticed his distraction.

The MC announced once more. "And now, let's give a shout-out to our Police and Firefighters."

The people cheered. Next, the MC called out the community's volunteer of the year. "Theda Strong." The people gave a standing ovation to the woman who baked pies for events and offered her ice cream shop and profits from July 4th to the police and firefighters. The MC handed her a gift card to a spa shop.

"Now, the towns' people wanted to give a special gift to Trevor Freeman for going above and beyond your duties and helping several people with their lawns, fixing faucets ..." and the list went on. People stood to applaud, but all the while Trevor stared down at his feet. Did they have to make it this big a deal? The whole thing was humiliating.

Thankfully, he didn't have to stand up in the midst of the uproar and excitement. The MC walked over to his table and handed him a gift card to some resort in Colorado Springs. He would probably end up using it to send his dad and sister there.

The servers began clearing dinner plates from the tables while the MC announced that dessert was going to be self-served.

People began moving around, and Trevor made small talk with Enrique while Rex caught up with some of his friends. Most people took advantage of dessert time to interact with each other, while some kids used the time to play tackle, chatter, or wrestle.

Trevor's gaze wandered back to Sofia's seat, but she wasn't there anymore. He turned his head to track her while Enrique talked until Enrique clapped his hands to bring Trevor back to the present.

Enrique gave him a knowing look.

"What?" Trevor asked in mock innocence.

"I said, what are you going to do about the pretty lady? Because at the end of the day, staring at her will not bring your lady back."

Trevor shrugged his shoulders. "That's what I've asked myself for the last two hours since I walked into the building."

Another person interrupted to talk to Enrique, and Trevor returned to their dinner table.

This time, he saw Sofia talking with her friend Chloe. Thankfully, Chloe had been a good ally during their separation. At least she'd managed to let Trevor know that Sofia had left, and had also shared the news of Sofia's salvation. Besides that, Chloe hadn't disclosed any other information about Sofia.

Trevor hadn't expected to see Sofia at all, especially today. Despite the town's tendency to gossip about everything from who was dating whom, who was new in town, and who had moved to where, rumors were scarce about what was going on with people who weren't as involved in the community, such as the Wises. The Wises always financially supported community events, but rarely made an appearance at any of them, which made it doubly surprising that all four of them had come to this dinner.

He leaned back in his chair and took a moment to study Sofia as she walked back to her family's table.

She looked stunningly beautiful in a flowing red dress that showed off her curves as if she'd just stepped off the red carpet.

Just looking at her again was a painful reminder of what a loser Trevor was, and what he used to have and let get away.

He ached to talk to her, to hug her. Her beaming smile was missing today. She looked tense, as if she

Rose Fresquez

were hurting too. Trevor knew he was the one responsible for her low spirits since he was the one who'd hurt her. He was hurting, too, but at least he deserved the pain since he'd put himself in that situation.

"You okay?"

He jerked his attention away from Sofia to see who'd interrupted his thoughts. "Yeah."

"You should go talk to her, Son," his dad said.

Trevor had contemplated doing just that a few times, but he didn't have the nerve to go near her family. What would they say if he walked up to her? That's if Sofia would even give him one second of her time. He at least had to apologize to her tonight, because he might not get another chance. He had no idea how long she was staying in Eron, or when he would be able to see her again. However, her presence tonight gave Trevor a glimmer of hope that their relationship could still be salvaged now that his mom's case had been laid to rest.

251

He wasn't sure how he would go about it, but Trevor was convinced that Sofia was the woman he wanted to spend the rest of his life with. He had to make things right between them, as well as between himself and her family. He couldn't let her go back to New York without making amends

"The longer you wait to say something, the less confidence you'll feel," his father said as he sat in a chair next to him.

Over the last few weeks, Rex had done his best not to interfere in Trevor's affairs, and Trevor appreciated that. He had let Trevor mourn his loss and lament his own stupidity without meddling. It was good to hear his words of encouragement once more after so long, although Trevor still needed to figure out a way to comfort Rex after the news about his wife.

With that little push from his father, Trevor found the courage to walk straight up to the Wise family, who were all laughing except for Sofia. It might have been easier for him to approach her while she was with Chloe instead of her family.

As if they were replaying their first meeting, everyone's laughter died down as soon as they spotted Trevor.

He paid no attention to the rest of the Wises—his eyes focused on Sofia. She looked amazing. Trevor didn't remember ever seeing anyone as beautiful as she was. It was almost like she hadn't gone through the same torment he had, but her demeanor showed otherwise.

Involuntarily, his hands started shaking, and he shoved them into his pockets so no one would notice.

"Yes, Detective, can we help you?" Jason Wise rose from his chair.

Trevor turned his gaze to the man, "Good day, sir, I…I again, I apologize for all the trouble I put you through and for erroneously thinking you had something to do with my mother's disappearance. I had no right to do that. It wasn't my place and I want to express how utterly sorry I am for everything." Trevor spoke with sincerity.

He figured he was going to be apologizing to this family for the rest of his life. Especially if he wanted to pursue one of them.

Jason nodded in acknowledgment of the words. His brows furrowed. "Anything else?"

Trevor's gaze locked with Sofia's, and for a few seconds, he held his breath. She looked away. It was now or never. He couldn't just leave this to chance. "I would also like to have a word with Sofia."

"And why is that?"

The man wasn't going to let him off easily. "I...want to apologize to her personally, and to let her know that I am still a work in progress. I would also like to have your blessing and permission to date her," Trevor stated, his voice gaining a confidence it hadn't had in years.

Trevor knew that Sofia didn't need her dad's blessing to go out with a man she chose, but he didn't want to have any clouds hanging over their relationship. That was, if Sofia would still take him back.

"Excuse me?" Marissa snapped as she rose from her seat, brows wrinkled.

Brent gave a sly chuckle. "You have some nerve. What kind of detective are you, anyway?" he sneered.

Blocking out Brent's words, Trevor continued to address Jason. As hard as it was dealing with this family, Jason surprisingly seemed the easiest one to talk to at the moment, probably since Trevor had had fewer run-ins with him at their home.

"I know that I'm not who you want for her, and if I were in your shoes, I would probably turn my nose up at myself, too, but I love her." If he hadn't gotten her attention before, those words were enough to grab Sofia's attention, and as her gaze flew to him, her eyes lit up. "That's all I have to offer her, but I love her with all my heart," he spoke, his eyes never straying from Sofia even once.

Jason's gaze flitted from Trevor to Sofia, as if he was assessing the situation. "As much as I have several reasons to not like you, I've enjoyed having my daughter back in my life and I would rather not interfere in her matters of the heart. I know that Sofia is a grown woman now, and I can't choose whom she dates."

Apparently, Jason Wise was of a different mind in that department than his wife. And Trevor was thankful for that.

"I suppose you two have a lot to talk about," Jason stated. "Come, Marissa." He motioned for his wife to join him.

Marissa opened her mouth and then closed it when her husband reached for her hand and dragged her. While walking away, she kept her angry stare on Sofia and Trevor until she almost ran into a wall.

Brent sent one of his threatening looks at Trevor, which didn't bother Trevor anymore. Not as long as Sofia was willing to talk to him. That was all Trevor cared about.

"Make it quick, Sofie." Brent glanced at the phone in his hand. "That's if you still plan to hitch a ride with me."

Brent walked away, and his sudden loud grunt and the sound of a dish clattering to the floor grabbed Trevor's and Sofia's attention. They both turned to see Keisha standing in front of Brent, her mouth open and eyes wide with terror.

"Great, this is so great!" Brent growled, his eyes glued to his chest.

It looked like Keisha had bumped into Brent and smothered his white shirt with a berry pie, and had gotten a few smudges on his sport coat, too. Trevor figured his timing couldn't get any worse.

"Oh no." Keisha clapped her hands to her trembling lips as Brent snarled viciously at her.

A few people who were not engaged in cleaning up watched curiously from a safe distance.

Brent pointed an accusing finger at Keisha. "Did your brother put you up to this?"

"I'm so sorry," Keisha stammered, her face flushed with embarrassment. She shook her head. "No, it was an accident. I'll buy you a new shirt and dry clean your coat."

Trevor knew he needed to stay calm and not act like a jerk toward Brent anymore, but his little sister didn't deserve to be traumatized by Brent's intimidating words. Keisha hated when Trevor intervened on her behalf, but she hadn't dealt with Brent Wise's fury before.

Trevor held Sofia's shoulders and stared at her warm green eyes. "I'm sorry. Will you please give me a minute?" Trevor asked Sofia, who nodded, then joined him as he moved closer to Brent and Keisha.

"I just wanted Sofia to try some of my berry cobbler," Keisha said in a subdued voice, her misty eyes on Sofia. "I'm sorry again, Mr. Wise."

Sofia stepped to Keisha's side and wrapped an arm around her shoulder. Brent glared at Keisha for a moment, then aggressively raked a hand through his neat blonde hair. Trevor waited for him to explode.

Instead, he looked Keisha up and down with a disgusted sneer, then grabbed some napkins from a nearby table to swipe ineffectively at his shirt. "You're getting a bill from me," he threatened through gritted teeth before he fled the scene. Keisha scooped up the mess on the floor with a broom someone handed her, then hurried away.

Once they were alone, Trevor and Sofia could only stare at each other, looking every bit like two awkward pre-teens. There was so much space in between them, so much tension filling that space. He had built up a wall to keep Sofia out until she finally left, but now here he was, walls down and heart exposed.

"You look ..." His eyes stared at the curls in her soft blond hair and then her dress.

Sofia's brows arched as if waiting for Trevor to finish.

"So beautiful tonight ... I mean, always, but your dress is lovely."

Just stop talking, Trevor, stop. Trevor thought to himself.

Sofia chuckled softly, which sent butterflies to Trevor's stomach, loosening all the knots it held. It was so good to see her smile, and for the first time in six weeks, Trevor smiled genuinely.

"Thanks."

"I…I..." Trevor began, interrupting Sofia as she started to speak at the same time.

He broke off and Sofia giggled nervously.

"You first," she said.

"I missed you, Sofia, and I didn't call you because I wanted to apologize to you in person. I'm so sorry for causing you any pain. You loved me regardless of my social status, and my differences with your family, yet all I ever did was push you away."

Sofia listened intently as Trevor spoke.

"I love you, Sofia Wise. You're everything to me."

Sofia didn't wait for Trevor's next words—she closed the distance between them and threw her arms around his neck, creating a jolt of excitement and anticipation for Trevor. Despite the audience around them, they forgot they weren't alone.

"I love you, too, and I missed you." She spoke with her head buried in his chest. She then took a small step back and lifted her head to look at him, keeping her palms pressed against his.

"Why should I believe that you won't break things off with me next time?" Sofia's face was a mixture of hope and doubt. "My family hasn't changed.

They still have money, and they're still jerks, although they are slowly coming around. "

Trevor didn't blame her for being skeptical. He cleared his throat. "Well, I was stupid and thought that love had a special league. But after you left, my life felt so incomplete without you. Things were not the same anymore. I ..." His throat felt like he was choking on glass. "I don't want to live without you, Sofia. In fact, I can't picture my future without you in it."

Sofia nodded in understanding, her eyes glistening. "Even though you'd said things were over between us, I never felt for a single moment that you were completely out of my life."

Trevor let out a heavy sigh of relief, and for the first time since he'd broken off things with Sofia, he felt like he could finally breathe. He still needed to share the details about his mom with her, but for now, this would have to do.

She stepped on tiptoes and kissed his forehead. Holding Trevor's hands, she said, "I need you to give me a few days, though, okay? I need to work things out with my family."

Trevor nodded. Although he didn't know what that meant, he felt hopeful. It was as if he'd been holding his breath underwater—as if he'd been drowning himself by shutting her out. Now that he'd finally broken through the surface, he wanted nothing more than to have Sofia now, but he knew he had to respect her wishes and give her time. After all, it had been his own choice that had separated them.

***

Sofia walked up to her brother, her spirits lifted after her discussion with Trevor. They had been quick about it, just like Brent wanted, especially after the pie episode.

"You know that Keisha didn't mean to stain your shirt, don't you?"

Brent's jaw tightened. "She doesn't seem to be a jerk like her brother, but you never know what they are plotting against me."

Deciding to make the matter lighter, Sofia shook her head and smiled. "You're a very interesting guy, you know that?"

Brents' gaze focused on the road and he shifted the gear into drive. He gripped the steering wheel so tightly that his knuckles were white.

"Glad I could amuse you, now that I'm the town's laughing stock." His jaw clenched, "I'm never going back to that cliché dinner again." He said through gritted teeth.

Sofia didn't want to have a heated conversation with her brother, especially not now, when her hope was to re-connect.

"How long are you staying in town?" Brent asked, taking her by surprise.

"I don't know yet. Another three weeks maybe?" She was still undecided, yet something inside her felt like she would stay a lot longer this time.

Hopefully, she and Trevor would be able to work things out and date as a normal couple. For now, she couldn't say if they would just pick up from where they left off, but she was eager to see how things would go from here. And it was even better that they didn't have to worry about his mother's disappearance anymore.

***

It was one week after Thanksgiving, and Sofia was meeting Chloe at Ricci's Italian Bistro for dinner.

As Sofia walked down the street, she pulled up the hood of her jacket to block the cold air from her ears. She could have parked her car closer to the restaurant, but she'd wanted a chance to admire the town's vibrancy. Lines of lights were strung downtown, and cheerful Christmas music boomed from most of the shops as she passed by. The petunia flower baskets she'd seen in the summer had been replaced by red and white poinsettias, and red bows hung over the shops. Everything emanated pure cheer and energy.

Sofia felt a thrill of excitement, more confirmation that she wanted to stay in this town, if not for any other reason than for the memories of her childhood and her grandma.

It was surprising that even though she'd spent the first fifteen years of her life in this town, she'd never had the chance to walk Main Street so freely on her own.

People waved and greeted her as they weaved in and out of the shops. She doubted they knew her, but they were just being friendly. Although she wouldn't be surprised if they did know who she was even though she didn't recognize them.

Sofia gave one more glance to the gently falling snowflakes floating out of the sky before she walked into the bistro. The bitter cold was replaced by the warmth in the building, and it felt comforting. The smell of homemade Italian foods filled Sofia's nostrils, which sent her tummy growling.

"So tell me, how did things go with Trevor?" Chloe asked eagerly as they sipped calming tea in the corner booth where they sat.

Sofia had needed to talk to someone else besides her family or Trevor. She filled Chloe in on the details of the day's events.

"He apologized and said he loved me in front of my dad and mom." Sofia placed a hand to her chest, eyes dreamy.

"What did your parents say, especially your mom?"

Social status had always been a big deal to Marissa since she'd grown up in poverty, and it was the same with Sofia's aunt, Jule's mom. "She wanted to say something, but my dad took her away." Sofia thought that her dad was coming around. He'd probably not felt like fighting with his daughter any more since their relationship was mending.

Her mother was still in that same phase as she always was where money mattered a great deal. Sofia couldn't blame her, since Marissa had grown up so poor, and when she landed Jason's wealth, she'd felt like she hit a lottery.

"Are you guys going to have a long distance relationship?"

Sofia's gaze was distant for a moment before she responded. "Actually, I'm considering moving back to Eron. I can work online, since I have a good assistant in New York," she added.

She took a breath and continued, "Trevor doesn't know yet, but... I want to stay. I have a lot to tell him, and can't wait to talk about spiritual things as a couple."

Sofia had asked Chloe to tell Trevor the news of her salvation. Although he'd not said anything to her. Sofia now understood that he'd been scared and struggling with the revelations about his mother's whereabouts.

Chloe stood up to embrace her friend. "I am so excited to have my friend back, and I'm happy for you and Trevor."

Since Sofia had never developed any other real friendships, she felt her heart leap. "Me, too."

"The guy upstairs from my shop is moving his stationery business to his house, so that place will be up for lease. Maybe you could start your real estate business," Chloe said. "You will be the first realtor who lives in town. If real estate is not something you want to do anymore, you can work with me here at the boutique. I would so love to have you here year-round."

Sofia flashed a triumphant grin, imagining herself joining Chloe on their less busy days, sitting in her comfy chairs as they talked. "I like that idea."

"Great!" Chloe said with excitement. "Did you know that Jules is moving back to Eron too?" Chloe's eyes twinkled.

Sofia felt a spark of excitement. Even though Chloe had been closer to Jules, Sofia would still be glad to see more of her cousin. "Is she really?"

Chloe nodded.

Sofia was slightly bothered that she'd lost touch with her cousin, but it was her own fault for not calling or texting. "I can't wait to see her again."

Sofia sipped her tea. She felt she'd been selfish, constantly talking about her personal life. "Enough about me. Anyone special in your life?"

Chloe smiled and shrugged. "Well, there's been interest from guys, but none have caught my attention at all, except this one cute guy…" Chloe winced.

"Why do I get the feeling you're not too excited about this 'guy'?" Sofia wiggled her fingers to indicate quotation marks.

"Well, I've gone out with him twice, after he kept asking me out for the last six months. Part of the reason is that he's so sweet. He helped mow my parent's lawn all summer long, and shovel their driveway ever since dad's back pain intensified." Chloe told Sofia she was considering giving the guy a chance. "Maybe I will get to like him that way."

Sofia propped her elbow on the table and rested her chin on her hand.

"Poor guy!" Sofia could relate since she'd gone on dates out of pity herself. She'd gone out with a colleague's' brother once just so she wouldn't hurt her friend's feelings. "So you're kind of being a Good Samaritan?"

Chloe smiled and waved off her comment.

Sofia took the time to soak in the interior of the restaurant. The lights were dim, and soft music played in the background. People were coming and going. The restaurant was filling up with the early dinner crowd. The bistro catered to all sorts of people.

Animated chatter rose from a few tables with occupants. It seemed to be a place for anyone. Both kids and adults loved Italian food, so this was the perfect place for family gatherings. The laughter of families filled the air from the row of booths. Some people were seated at the bar stools by the cash registers. It was a perfect evening crowd for a small town.

Sofia had noticed a gentleman seated two tables across from them. He sat alone, but his eyes kept darting to their table, and if she wasn't mistaken, he was staring at Chloe, and Chloe had stared back a few times.

The guy's eyes went back to his plate whenever Sofia caught him staring.

Sofia turned to Chloe and whispered, "Do you know that the cute guy over there has been checking you out the entire time?"

Chloe chuckled softly, as if aware of what Sofia was talking about, but then her eyes went to the gentleman's table. When their eyes met, the guy smiled and waved to Chloe. Though she looked embarrassed that she'd been caught, she returned the wave, then turned back to Sofia. "Oh, oh."

"Do you know him?" Sofia asked.

She shook her head. "I heard rumors that there's a new heartbreaker guy in town," Chloe said.

"Does everyone know everything around here?"

Chloe nodded. "For the most part, yes. Stephanie at Theda's ice cream shop spreads news really fast. She and another girl are trying to get an Eron Facebook group going. For now, Stephanie posts most of the community pictures on Instagram. I'm surprised they haven't posted a picture of him yet." The waitress showed up with their dinner.

"Speaking of posts," Chloe spoke again. "You made the Eron Tribune, and you're on the town's web page. 'POWER COUPLE.'

Sofia's jaw dropped.

Chloe nodded, moving a fork through her pasta as steam rose from it. "Someone managed to take your picture at some point when you had your hands wrapped around Trevor's neck, while you kissed his forehead. Rumor has it it's going on the new Facebook page as the banner." She pointed a fork towards Sofia. "Thanks for modeling in one of my designer dresses by the way. It's a great advertisement for my upcoming fashion show."

"People need to get a life in this town," Sofia said.

"That's the life they have, girl. Welcome to Eron."

Chloe took another sip of her tea, which spilled on her chest.

"I am definitely not going to look at the guy again," Chloe whispered to Sofia as she opted for a glass of water instead of tea this time. Thankfully, the waitress chose that moment to take their dessert orders.

***

Trevor had kept extra busy for the last week, something unusual in Eron, especially during the holidays. He'd been off today since he'd switched a shift with Scott, but he'd still received two calls to help some of the citizens in town. He'd checked his cell phone several times in between calls, in case Sofia had contacted him. But she hadn't, and he was debating whether to text her before he went to his next supposedly off-duty assignment in directing construction traffic.

Sofia had said she needed some time to work things out with her family. And despite Trevor's urge to see her, he told himself she deserved the space. Trevor wondered how much time she needed. But then again, the least he could do after what he'd done to her was to give her as much time as she needed.

Gazing at the trees, which were covered with ice as thick as Christmas cake frosting, Trevor could hardly imagine that just a week ago, the last leaves of Fall had been fluttering from rough, bare twigs.

He adjusted his scarf, wishing he'd remembered to bring his earmuffs. Even though he'd grown up in

Eron, he'd never adjusted to the winter weather. It didn't help when he had to be directing traffic on days like today.

He'd been called in as backup, since they needed an extra cop. The freeze had broken some water pipes on Highway 92, and he'd been called in as backup, since they'd needed an extra cop to guide drivers around the construction workers who were doing the repairs.

As he continued to direct traffic, his mind was far from what he was doing, but he still recognized a few faces from Eron. "Detective, what's up?" one of the locals called from his truck.

Trevor greeted one of the farmers from town with a wave. "Hi, Mojo!"

Mojo's truck was loaded with hay. "Why are they doing construction in the middle of the day?"

Trevor moved towards the old man's truck and leaned in the window to explain. "Busted pipe, but it should be done in two hours." Trevor doubted it would be two hours, since there were only two people performing a task for four.

The screeching of tires caused him to turn his eyes back to the road, where a minor collision had taken place.

"See you later, Mojo." He waved goodbye as the sixty-something-year-old drove off.

The vehicles involved were a BMW and a pickup truck. *Oh, no*, thought Trevor. He recognized that BMW. He dreaded what awaited him as he approached.

It was Brent Wise, of course, and Pete Haldem. Pete was tall and very muscular, in his late 30's, and Trevor had arrested him a few times for starting fights. Pete didn't hold it against him, and he and Trevor had managed to become friends anyway. Despite Pete's aggressive attitude, he was a hard-working man who'd fought for everything he had, but patience was not in his nature. Pete had returned from the military three years ago with a severe case of PTSD. His time in the service had taken a lot out of him, and he didn't care what he did, and most of the town's people knew better than to mess with him.

Trevor hoped Brent would tread lightly with the guy that loomed high above him. He was a strong man, and a match for Brents' attitude.

"You scratched my car," Brent sneered, passing a finger over the small dent on the passenger side of his BMW.

"Boy, if you care so much about your car, you need to obey the traffic rules." Pete spoke fiercely and his sharp eyes looked ready to cut through glass. His hands were already balled into fists at his side, his bitterness consuming him.

"Okay guys, we're holding up traffic," Trevor said, hoping to diffuse the situation, but his words were quickly cut off.

"You're gonna have to pay to get this fixed," Brent said, ignoring Trevor completely. He inched into

Pete's personal space and jabbed a finger in the man's face, nearly poking him in the eye.

"Don't point a finger to my face, boy!" Pete took a step forward to slap Brent's hand away. "You're the one at fault here. "

Attempting to assert his authority again, Trevor spoke more loudly this time, to talk above their raised voices. "Lets' drive further so we can assess the situation to the side."

At this point, Pete had already drawn back his fist to throw a punch at Brent. Trevor was relieved when he froze mid-punch and relaxed ever so slightly. Brent was more mouth than muscle, and a punch was not what he needed.

Trevor grabbed Pete's fist and held it firmly while he stared him in the eye. "Hey, you don't want to do this, okay?" Trevor knew that Pete would only get sued by Brent and would end up losing anyway. He thought he'd succeeded in cooling Pete down when the man unclenched his jaw and took a deep breath, and started to lower his fist. Trevor released his grip and took half a step back.

"Let him hit me and see what happens!" Brent taunted, now that there was some distance between him and the bigger man. "Just because you act all macho, don't think you can mess with just anyone.

Pete changed his mind that instant. Trevor saw the fist heading Brent's way and quickly stepped in between the two men, which earned him a sharp punch straight to his forehead.

Blood gushed as the skin on his forehead split open. Trevor hit the ground, his head spinning. Through the haze, he heard Brent curse, then a car door slamming, which told him at least Brent was smart enough to get into his BMW.

The cold, hard ground was uncomfortable. Thankfully, it wasn't snowing, but the wind was freezing. He struggled to get to his feet and Pete gave him a hand, apologizing over and over. He could tell Pete felt horrible about it. Both men finally moved their damaged vehicles to the side and exchanged insurance information in a semi-civil manner.

Trevor rubbed his fingers and thumb over his forehead at the headache forming—which wasn't a great feeling when guiding traffic. He pushed through anyway, since Enrique needed to be on standby for the other calls. He called Scott to take over as soon as possible, so he could get himself to the ER.

***

After his visit to Eron's small clinic, Trevor drove back home with a bandage covering a row of stitches on his forehead. Exhaustion clung to him.

He tried to relax as he sat in his living room, nursing his wound. The doctor had instructed him to apply an ice pack every 15-20 minutes to reduce the swelling above his left eye.

Their Christmas tree had been set up in the corner, with the box of ornaments underneath, still untouched. At least they'd already strung the Christmas lights. Keisha added a few logs to the fireplace to make the room more warm and cozy.

"Can I get you anything, Trev?" Keisha asked as she slid onto the sofa by his side. Trevor held an ice pack to his forehead with one hand and held the remote in the other so he could flip through the channels.

"Thanks, Ki, I'm okay." His sister had pampered him and made sure he'd been comfortable. He couldn't ask for a better sister, even if he wanted to.

"Brent didn't even offer you a ride after you took a punch for him?" Keisha's voice was filled with disbelief. "I'm glad you didn't embarrass me in front of him. Thanks for letting me handle him in my own way."

That was quite an understatement, since Trevor had almost interceded when Brent had roared at Keisha for accidentally bumping into him. If Keisha considered shivering in front of Brent a way of dealing with him, then Trevor had to give his sister extra credit for patience.

Keisha's gaze lingered on the flames, her thoughts clearly distant. "I bet Brent has a good heart deep down somewhere. Maybe no one has given him a reason to love, and feel compassion for others." Keisha chuckled softly, "Mallory is not the best sidekick for him, either."

Trevor felt a pang of guilt, realizing that he was God's instrument to reach Brent, but he'd failed terribly.

"I could have done better with Brent," Trevor admitted. "I'm glad he didn't offer me a ride. I doubt I would have agreed to ride with him anyway," Trevor said with a soft chuckle. "The guy hates my guts, and for a good reason." Trevor placed the remote on the coffee table after settling on a reality show where people survived in the wilderness. He propped his feet on the table and leaned back on the couch. "What are the chances he wouldn't drive me out in the woods and tie me to a tree where no one could find me?"

Keisha started to laugh hard, but the laughter faded suddenly, causing Trevor to turn his head. His gaze found the one person he'd least expected, yet most wanted to see. Sofia was in their tiny living room, a tote bag dangling from her hand.

His heart raced, the way it always did at the sight of her. He lowered his feet from the table and fidgeted in his seat until Keisha came to the rescue, rising from the three-person couch.

"Hi, Sofia!" Keisha said, breaking the silence.

"Your dad was in the front yard. He told me to come in." Sofia bit her lip. "I hope I'm not interrupting anything."

Interrupting? Was she kidding? The only thing she was interrupting was his heart rate. Trevor was sure his blood pressure had gone up a notch or two.

He assumed it must be around five, if his dad was already home. He had lost track of time given the circumstances.

"You will never interrupt me, Sofia," Trevor managed, his voice shaky.

Keisha gestured Sofia to her previous seat next to Trevor. "Please have a seat."

"I brought you dinner," Sofia said, handing off the tote to Keisha.

"You cook?" Keisha asked in surprise as she accepted the bag.

"I do, but I haven't done so in such a long time, being last minute, I stopped by Ricci's."

"Thanks!" Keisha said as she made her way to the kitchen.

Trevor was still numb, as if his hand had frozen holding the ice pack to his head. Sofia was so close to him that their legs were touching.

"How are you feeling?" she whispered. He could feel the warm air from her mouth, and the soft scent of her body spray or shampoo, whatever it was, filled the air.

Rumor traveled fast in this town, but he doubted Sofia had gotten the news from the local grapevine this fast, since she didn't come into town often.

"I think I'll survive, now that you're here." His face creased with a smile. Sofia took the ice pack from his forehead and gasped at the sight of his wound.

Her eyes widened. "Oh my gosh, are you okay?"

Trevor Chuckled. "Never felt better."

She stared at him with an intense gaze and smiled. "You're pretty cool, you know that?" She put the ice pack gently back to his face and held it there for him. "You could have let my brother get hit. Perhaps he needs to learn a lesson or two somehow."

"How did you know?"

"Well, Chloe texted me, and then I had to ask Brent if you were okay. I got into this huge fight with Brent, because I told him he was so self-centered." She shrugged. "I called him some other names, too, of course, since he didn't give you a ride."

"I was fine, and I would have turned him down. Can you imagine me sitting in the car with your brother for longer than five minutes?" Trevor grinned, just thinking of how his time would have gone in Brent's BMW.

"Don't be upset with Brent, he's okay. I probably haven't given him a reason to be on his good side either," Trevor said sincerely.

Now that Sofia was holding the ice on his head, Trevor was glad he took the punch instead of Brent. It was worth it to avoid the hassle of having to visit Sofia at their mansion. Her hands felt so right on him, and the fact that they were both on the couch made him feel like they were a married couple. He definitely wanted to have this—coming home to her after a long day, and relaxing on the couch with the woman he loved.

He wondered where their relationship was headed. She was going right back before Christmas, as far as he knew. The town needed him, but he needed Sofia. They could hire another officer. His sister was graduating from high school next spring. It was a good time for her to become more independent, with their dad to look after her.

"What's on your busy detective mind?" Sofia asked after a long silence.

"I want to come to New York with you."

Sofia's jaw dropped, and she took the ice pack off his face.

"What?" Confused, she asked, "Why?"

"Marry me, Sofia. I don't have a ring right now..." His mouth opened and closed, then opened again. "These last few weeks since you left for New York made me realize how much I want you to be a part of my life and want to see you every day. I really love you, Sofia, and I don't want to spend another day without you."

"But your family is everything to you."

"I know, but you will be a part of me, and I love my family, but I want you to be my wife and my family. I will go where you go, as long as we're together."

Trevor could see tears gleaming in Sofia's eyes, reflecting the soft lights from the Christmas tree. He hoped they were tears of joy. He knew it was absolutely crazy to be proposing to her. They had just reconnected, yet the words felt right, as if he was being guided to say them.

"I want to marry you, Trevor." She rose from her seat onto his lap and wrapped her arms around him, kissing his cheek several times.

Realizing she had even used his name instead of detective, they both smiled. His name sounded so right on her lips.

"But I don't want you to come to New York," she added.

Trevor frowned, confused.

"I want to stay here in Eron with you and your family. Oh, Trevor..." She dropped her head to his.

"Sofia ..." He tucked her hair behind her ear and whispered in a hoarse voice. "You've fully captured my heart."

He took a moment to inhale her sweet scent, never wanting to let her go. She was warm and sweet, and when his fingers raked into her hair, he kissed her possessively with a passion like none before, all while thanking God for the punch and the case that had landed him the girl.

"And if it's okay, I see a Christmas tree in the corner that needs decorating. Perhaps I can help decorate it with you, Keisha and your dad?"

"That would be the best Christmas present," Trevor said.

Sofia shook her head. "No, it will be my best Christmas. My first Christmas as a follower of Christ and being engaged to the love of my life. How can I top that?"

Trevor couldn't argue with that, and they both shared a comfortable silence.

Keisha stepped in carrying a tray with eggnog, a bottle of sparkling cider, and some pastries she'd made earlier.

"Sorry to eavesdrop, but I think we have a reason to celebrate tonight."

Startled, Sofia tried to jerk herself off Trevor's lap, but he pulled her back to stay.

Rex walked in with a tray of disposable champagne flute glasses, and clear glasses for their eggnog.

After Keisha had filled glasses with sparkling cider, Rex lifted his glass. "To welcome Sofia to the family, and to my son. Congratulations, you two."

"Thanks, Dad," Trevor said, his lungs expanding to their fullest as he took in a deep breath.

"Congratulations," Keisha rubbed her hands together, smiling, "I can't wait to have another girl around. I'm so excited to have the coolest sister-in-law."

Sofia beamed. Setting her glass down, she walked to Keisha and embraced her. "I can't wait to spend time with you, Keisha."

Trevor was the happiest man alive. What had started out as a quest to find his missing mother had landed him in a far more complicated mystery—investigating his feelings for Sofia Wise.

With all the complex obstacles that had come between them from the start, Trevor had no idea how he deserved to end up with her. All he knew was that he'd somehow captured the girl who had stolen his heart. Case closed.

IF YOU ENJOYED READING THIS BOOK, PLEASE LEAVE A REVIEW.
Honest reviews by readers like yourself help bring attention to books. A review can be as short or as detailed as you like. Thank you so much!

Come back to Eron and read

Chloe and Zach's story in,

CHOICES

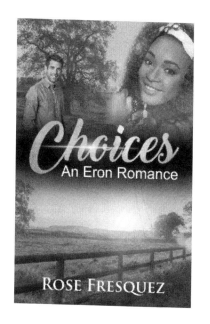

Chloe has finally returned home to stay, embracing the simple lifestyle of Eron. She opens her own fashion boutique and is contemplating a relationship with a guy who has plans to start a family. Chloe's own plans to settle for her local suitor are disrupted when a charming doctor walks into her boutique, opening up new dating options.

Dr. Zach has never been a man to settle in one place. When Zach's unknown grandparents leave him a house in Colorado on forty acres of land. Eron is supposed to be just another quick stop. That is, until the town's only doctor gets hurt.

When the town starts depending on him for their medical needs, Zach finds himself getting more involved in the town than he'd bargained for. Especially when he falls for the beautiful fashion designer who knows more about his grandparents than he'd expected.

Zach is forced to make a tough decision between his old life and a place full of new possibilities. A place that just might be home.

ABOUT THE AUTHOR

Rose Fresquez weaves Christian Interracial Romances. She has also written two Family Devotions. She leaves in the Rocky Mountains with her husband, and their four children. When she's not busy taking care of her family, she's writing.

You can connect with Rose online:

Website

Facebook

Goodreads

 Book Bub.

Twitter

To hear about future releases, subscribe to her Newsletter! which is usually sent out twice a month with free reads from other authors and random drawings just for fun.

Alternatively, email her at rjfresquez@gmail.com

Made in the USA
Columbia, SC
27 April 2022